Anonymous

The Children's Picture Fable-book

Containing One Hundred andSixty Fables

Anonymous

The Children's Picture Fable-book
Containing One Hundred andSixty Fables

ISBN/EAN: 9783744792349

Printed in Europe, USA, Canada, Australia, Japan

Cover: Foto ©Andreas Hilbeck / pixelio.de

More available books at **www.hansebooks.com**

THE CHILDREN'S
PICTURE FABLE-BOOK

CONTAINING

ONE HUNDRED AND SIXTY FABLES

With Sixty Illustrations by Harrison Weir.

BOSTON
TICKNOR AND FIELDS.
MDCCCLX.

LIST OF ILLUSTRATIONS.

THE CHILDREN'S
PICTURE FABLE-BOOK.

B

THE CHILDREN'S
F A B L E - B O O K.

THE FOX AND THE GOAT.

A Fox was one day drinking at a well when his feet slipped and he fell into the water. It was not deep enough to drown him, yet, with all his efforts, poor Reynard could not get out. Presently a thirsty Goat looked in, and seeing the Fox at the bottom, asked him if the water was good. "Oh, yes," said the Fox, "it is beautiful, and there is plenty of it." In jumped the Goat, and in a moment the

THE FOX AND THE GOAT.

Fox leaped on to his back, and thence out of the well. "Aha, my friend!" said he, as he stood in safety on the brink, "if your brains had been equal to your beard you'd have looked before you leaped!" and then the cunning fellow ran away and left the poor Goat in the water.

Before you follow the advice of cunning people think well of the consequences.

THE BIRDS, THE BEASTS, AND THE BAT.

ONCE upon a time a fierce Battle was fought between the Birds and the Beasts. The

Bat, taking advantage of his two-fold nature, kept hovering about from one side to the other as he saw either of them prevail. At one time the Beasts, under their leader the Lion, caused the Birds to take to flight; and then the Bat joined them; and when the Birds, having rallied under their general the Eagle, scattered the Beasts, then the Bat was found in the ranks of the Birds. At length peace was concluded, and the conduct of the Bat having been taken into consideration, he was condemned by both parties, and was obliged to betake himself to flight; and ever since then he has been skulking in holes and corners during the day, and only venturing out in the dusk of the evening.

The fickle-minded are not to be trusted.

THE FOX AND THE GRAPES.

ONE fine day in autumn a Fox crept into a garden where the ripe Grapes were hanging in beautiful clusters from the trellis-work against a sunny wall. He sat and looked at them with longing eyes, and at last jumped up and snapped at the lowest bunch; but, alas! it was beyond his reach. He tried again, and then again, but with no better success; and at length finding that his attempts were all in vain, he tossed up his head and walked away, muttering to himself, "Why should I trouble myself about them?—the Grapes are sour."

When boys try for a prize at school and don't succeed, they often pretend that it's not worth the having.

The Fox and the Grapes.

THE BOYS AND THE FROGS.

A NUMBER of heedless Boys were one day playing by the side of a pond; and seeing that it contained a great number of Frogs, they began to pelt them with stones. They had killed several of them, when an old Frog, the father of some of the lost ones, raised his head above the water and cried out, "Stop your sport, boys! this may be play to you, but it is death to us."

Never give pain to others, even in sport.

THE OLD HOUND.

An Old Hound, who had for many years done good service in the field, and who had been a great favourite with his master, at length, through old age, had become feeble and well-nigh useless. One day in the chase he attempted to seize a Stag, but his old teeth not being strong enough to hold the animal, it escaped. Upon this the Master came up in a violent passion and was about to strike him, when the faithful creature thus pleaded: "Hold thine hand, master; it is not my will, but my strength, which is wanting. Think of my past services, and do not punish my present failings."

The services of faithful servants should never be forgotten.

THE DOG AND THE SHADOW.

A Dog was crossing a rivulet with a piece of meat which he had just stolen from a butcher's stall, when, on looking into the stream, he saw, as he supposed, another Dog with another piece of meat in his mouth; and desiring to possess that also, he made a snap at it, when, lo and behold! the bit he was carrying dropped into the water, and immediately sank to the bottom.

Never give up a certainty for an uncertainty.

THE DOG AND THE SHADOW.

THE COUNTRYMAN AND THE SNAKE.

ONE cold frosty winter morning a Countryman happened to see under a hedge a Snake almost dead with cold. Having compassion on it, he placed it in his bosom, brought it home, and laid it by the fire. The warmth soon restored it; but the first use it made of its regained strength was to erect itself and fly at the wife and children of its preserver. Upon this the Countryman seized a mattock, and laid the animal dead at his feet.

It is the nature of ungrateful people to return evil for good.

THE OLD WOMAN AND HER MAIDS.

An Old Woman had two Maids whom she called every morning to get to their work at the crowing of the Cock. The Maids were very fond of their bed; and thinking that the Cock was the cause of their being obliged to rise so early, they determined to wring its neck, so that their Mistress would not be able to tell what time it was. But they had no sooner done this, than the Old Woman, afraid lest she should oversleep herself and thereby allow her Maids to lie too long in bed, was constantly rousing them, even at midnight.

In flying from lesser evils we often rush into greater.

THE LION AND THE MOUSE.

ONE day, as a Lion was sleeping in his
den, a Mouse scampered over the nose of
the Royal Beast. The Lion, thus aroused
from his sleep, clapped his paw on the
little intruder, and was just about to put
him to death, when the Mouse begged of
him in piteous tones to spare his life, and
not to stain his noble character with the
blood of so small and insignificant an
animal. The Lion, amused at the fright
of the little creature, at once let him go.
A short time after this, the Lion, while
ranging the woods in search of his prey,
was caught in the snare of the hunter.
He tried with all his strength to get free,
but not being successful he set up such a
roar as made the whole forest echo again.

THE LION AND THE MOUSE.

The Mouse, hearing the voice, and recognising it as that of his former friend, ran to the spot, and told the Lion that he would soon release him. He then set to work, and with his sharp little teeth gnawed asunder the fastenings of the snare, and set the Lion at liberty.

A kind action is never thrown away.

THE WANTON CALF.

A Calf, full of fun and play, was permitted to run wild in the fields; and as he had never himself felt the yoke, one day when he saw an Ox at plough, he could not refrain from insulting him. " What a poor drudge you are," said he, "with that heavy yoke about your neck. What a much happier life I lead! I run and frisk about where I please, sometimes in the cool shade, and sometimes in the open sunshine; and when I feel thirsty, I go to the clear, sweet brook. Really I pity you from the bottom of my heart!" The Ox paid no heed to his remarks, but went on calmly with his work. Some time after this the Ox saw the Calf taken out of the field, and led away by a priest to be sacrificed. "Now," said the Ox to him, "you see the end of your idleness and insolence. It was for this only that you were suffered to live. I think that my work is better than your play, and that my condition is to be preferred to yours."

Seek not what is most pleasant, but what is most useful.

c

THE COCK AND THE JEWEL.

As a young Cock was seeking for food for himself and his Hens in a farmyard, he happened to scratch up a bright, glittering Jewel, which by some accident had been dropped there. Not seeing what use such an article could be to him, he pretended to despise it; so, shaking his head very wisely, he said, " You may be a very fine thing to those who can value you, but for my part my taste lies in quite another direction. I would rather have a barley-corn than all the jewels in the world."

The Ignorant often undervalue what they do not understand.

THE COCK AND THE JEWEL.

HERCULES AND THE WAGONER.

As a Countryman was driving a heavily laden wagon along a miry lane, the wheels stuck so fast in the clay that the horses could not draw them out.   Whereupon the man, without making any effort of his own, began to pray to Hercules to come and help him.   But Hercules told him that he was an idle fellow, and bade him exert himself, apply his whip to the horses, and put his shoulder to the wheel, for the Gods only helped those who helped themselves.

"I will try," has wrought wonders.

THE OAK AND THE WILLOW.

AFTER a very stormy night a father and son went into the field to see what damage the storm had caused. The son said, " Look, father, there is the strong Oak-tree lying yonder on the ground ; while the slender Willow stands as upright as ever. I should have thought that the Willow would have been uprooted, and not the proud Oak, which has lived so many years." " My son," answered the father, " the Oak was broken, because it fought against the storm ; while the Willow, by yielding to the gale, avoided its fury, and still lives."

Better bend than break.

THE FOX AND THE CROW.

A Crow having taken a piece of cheese from a cottage window, flew with her prize to the bough of a tree where she intended to enjoy it at her leisure. A sly Fox having observed her, came and sat at the foot of the tree, planning how he might cheat her out of the tempting morsel. "Bless me, my dear Mrs. Crow!" began the Fox; "I am surprised that thy exceeding loveliness never struck me before,— how perfect is thy form,— how bright and glossy thy plumage,— and what a graceful attitude! I have never heard thy sweet voice, but if it equals the beauty of thy body it must indeed be charming." The Crow, tickled with this flattery, wrig-

THE FOX AND THE CROW.

gled and twisted herself about, and desiring to enlighten the Fox on the point on which he seemed to be doubtful, opened her mouth with the intention of sending forth a musical caw, when—down dropped the cheese, which was at once snapped up by the Fox, who trotted off, laughing to himself at the success of his plan and at the simplicity of the Crow.

Never listen to flatterers.

THE HUSBANDMAN AND THE STORK.

A HUSBANDMAN, wishing to protect his new-sown corn from the Cranes, set a net in his field to catch them. One morning he took several, and among their number there happened to be a Stork. " Spare my life," cried the Stork; " I am no thieving Crane; I am, as you see, a poor, harmless, innocent Stork, the most pious and dutiful of all birds. I always honour and help my parents; I am ever attending to their wants. I——" " That may all be very well," interrupted the Husbandman, " but seeing that I have caught you in the company of those who were destroying my corn, you must suffer with them." And with these words he wrung the Stork's neck.

Avoid bad company.

THE DOG IN THE MANGER.

A CHURLISH Dog lay in a manger full of hay; and when a hungry Ox came near wishing to eat his food, the ill-natured cur began to snarl and bite at him. " What a selfish animal thou art!" said the Ox; " thou canst not eat the hay thyself, nor wilt thou suffer others to partake of it."

Selfishness is always despised.

THE DOG IN THE MANGER.

THE ASS AND THE LAPDOG.

A CERTAIN Man had an Ass and a Lapdog. He was a kind master to them. The Ass, it is true, had to work hard in drawing wood and water, but he had a comfortable stable and plenty of good hay to eat. The Lapdog accompanied his master in all his walks, frisking and skipping about him; and when at home he was allowed to lie in his lap. The Ass, becoming discontented with his lot, thought that he too would be fondled and caressed if he imitated the actions of the Dog. So one day he followed his master into the house, and commenced to gambol and caper about in a very awkward manner. The master at first could not help laughing at the strange antics of the Ass; but he soon found that it was no joke. The Ass continued to jump about, damaging the furniture, and breaking the crockery; and approaching closer to him, the stupid creature at length began to paw him with his heavy feet, and to show an inclination to get into his lap. This was too much—the master called loudly for assistance, when his servants entered, and so belaboured the silly animal with their heavy sticks, that they soon proved to him that an Ass is not at all times to be desired as a companion.

Presumption and impertinence generally meet their due punishment.

THE STAG AT THE POOL.

ONE very sultry day, a Stag, while quench-
ing his thirst at a pool of clear water, saw
his form reflected in the stream. "Ah!"
said he, "what glorious antlers these
are,—how gracefully they tower above
my head! I wish that the rest of my body
were equal to them. But really I feel
quite ashamed of these thin, weak, slender
legs of mine." While thus musing, suddenly the horn of the huntsman and the
baying of the hounds were heard. Away
flies the Stag, and by the aid of his despised legs he soon outruns his pursuers;
but taking the direction of a forest, he
had the misfortune to be entangled by
his horns among some branches, where he
was held till the hounds came up and

THE STAG AT THE POOL.

pulled him down.   He now saw what a mistake he had made in speaking so slightingly of those legs which would have carried him out of danger, and in being so vain of those horns which had caused his ruin.

The useful is to be preferred to the beautiful.

THE BEAR AND THE BEE-HIVES.

As a Bear was clambering over a fence to a place where there were some Bee-hives, he upset one of them and began to take away the honey.   The Bees immediately set upon him to avenge this insult; and though their little stings could not pierce his thick shaggy hide, yet they fastened about his nostrils and eyes, and caused him so much pain, that in trying to dislodge them he tore all his face with his claws, and suffered a just punishment for the injury he had done the Bees in breaking their waxen cells.

Never irritate a multitude.

THE THIRSTY PIGEON.

ONE hot summer's day, a Pigeon, parched with thirst, saw upon a painted sign a glass of water, and supposing it to be real, she dashed with such force against it that she broke her wing and fell to the ground, where she was quickly taken by a passer-by.

Take care, or care will take you.

THE WAR-HORSE AND THE ASS.

A WAR-HORSE, adorned with military trappings, came thundering along the road, making the ground ring again with the sound of his trampling hoofs. A patient Ass happened at the time to be slowly trudging along the same road with a heavy load on his back. The Charger loudly ordered the poor Ass to get out of his way, or he would tread him under his feet. The Ass, not wishing to quarrel with the Horse, meekly stepped on one side, and allowed him to go by. Not long after this, the Horse was sent to the wars, and was there badly wounded, and being no longer fit for military service, he was stripped of all his fine ornaments and sold to a farmer. The next time the Ass saw the

THE WAR-HORSE AND THE ASS.

Horse, the latter was with great effort dragging a cart; and the Ass then understood what little cause he had to envy one who in prosperity had treated with contempt those whom he considered his inferiors.

Pride must have a fall.

THE LION IN LOVE.

As a Lion was roaming through the forest he happened to see the Woodman's daughter tripping lightly along, and fell in love with her at first sight. So violent was his passion that he at once demanded her of her father in marriage. The Wood-

man was not at all pleased with this proposal, but remembering the power and the
strength of the suitor, he thought it would
be best to pretend to consent to it. " I
assure your Majesty," said the man, " that
I feel highly flattered with your kind
intentions towards my daughter; but seeing she is so tender and delicate, might I
ask of you to permit me to draw those
great teeth and to cut off those sharp claws
of yours?" The Lion, too much in love
to hesitate, allowed the man to do as he
pleased; but no sooner had the Woodman
deprived the Lion of his claws and teeth
than he seized a thick cudgel and drove
him back into the woods.

*Never allow your feelings to get the better
of your discretion.*

THE WOLF AND THE LAMB.

ONE very hot day a Wolf and a Lamb happened to come together to quench their thirst at a clear, silvery brook that ran down by the side of a mountain. The Wolf took his stand upon the higher ground, and the Lamb at some distance farther down the stream. The Wolf, seeing that the Lamb was fat and plump, determined to pick a quarrel with her. " What do you mean," said the Wolf, glaring upon the Lamb with his fierce eyes, " by making the water so muddy, that I cannot possibly drink it?" The Lamb mildly replied, " I cannot see how that can be, as the water runs from you to me, not from me to you." " That may be," said the Wolf, in a tone of anger, " but I have been told that six months ago

THE WOLF AND THE LAMB.

you used impertinent language towards me."
"Really," answered the Lamb, "you must
be mistaken, as at that time I was not born."
The Wolf upon this fell into a dreadful
passion, and drawing closer to the Lamb,
said, "Well, if it were not you, it must
have been some of your family; so it is all
the same,—and just now I am in want of
my supper." So saying he leapt at the
throat of the poor innocent Lamb, and tore
her in pieces.

*Never act the tyrant towards those
weaker and younger than yourself, or you
will be likened to the Wolf in this Fable.*

THE FLIES AND THE POT OF HONEY.

A POT of Honey having been upset in a grocer's shop, the Flies, according to their custom of rushing upon sweet things, settled in swarms upon it. When they had had their fill, and wished to fly away, they found that they were not able, for their feet had stuck so fast in the honey, that the more they tried to get away, the more their wings became clogged, and they at length became stifled in the sweets around them.

A life of pleasure often terminates in misery and ruin.

THE EAGLE AND THE JACKDAW.

An Eagle swooped down from a lofty rock upon a Lamb, and bore off his prize high into the air. A Jackdaw, who was sitting on the branches of an elm, thought that he could do the same; so having selected a Sheep for his prey, he came down with all his force on to its back; but his claws becoming entangled in the wool, in his struggles to free himself he made such a cawing and fluttering that he attracted the notice of the Shepherd, who coming up, easily captured him, clipped his wings, and took him home to amuse his family.

Do not attempt to do that which is beyond your strength.

THE EAGLE AND THE JACKDAW.

THE BUNDLE OF STICKS.

A FATHER had seven Sons who were always quarrelling with one another. This distressed the Father very much. One day he desired all of them to come to his chamber. He there laid before them seven sticks which were fastened together. "Now," said he, "I will give a hundred crowns to that one of you who can break this Bundle of Sticks asunder." Each of them tried to the utmost of his strength, and each was obliged to confess that he could not break it. "And yet," said the Father, "there is no difficulty about it." He then untied the bundle, and broke one stick after the other with the greatest ease. Then he said, "As it is with these sticks, my sons, so it is with you. As long as you hold together, you are a match for all your enemies; but if you quarrel and separate, it will happen to you as to these sticks which you see lying broken on the ground."

Union is strength.

THE CRAB AND HIS MOTHER.

ONE day as a young Crab and his Mother were taking a walk, the Mother said, " Why do you not walk straight, my son?—your legs look quite crooked!" " Mother," said the son, "when I see you walking straight, I shall be happy to follow your example."

Example is better than precept.

THE FROGS WHO DESIRED
A KING.

In olden times when the Frogs ranged in liberty over the ponds and lakes, they grew weary of their tame mode of life; and desiring some change, they assembled together, and with no little noise besought Jupiter to send them a King to keep them in better order. Jupiter was much amused at the petition of the Frogs, and with a view to humour them, he threw into their midst a Log, saying, "There is a King for you!" The sudden fall of the Log caused a mighty splash, which sent all the Frogs hither and thither; and it was some time before any of them ventured to take a peep at their new lord and master. At length some of the more courageous among them

THE FROGS DESIRING A KING.

swam towards him, where they were soon
followed by the rest; and seeing that there
was no motion in him, they leaped upon his
back, and capered and danced upon him
with the greatest contempt for his majesty.
Such a King did not at all please them;
they, therefore, again sent messengers to Jupiter to petition for a King who had some
life, motion, and activity in him. Whereupon Jupiter sent a Stork, saying he hoped
this would suit them. The Stork no sooner
came among his new subjects than he began
to devour them one after the other as fast
as he possibly could. The second King
being even less to their liking than the first,
the Frogs immediately sent Mercury with a
private message to Jupiter beseeching him to
have mercy upon them, and either to grant
them another King or restore them to their
former condition. But Jupiter would not
listen to them. "No," said he, "it was

their own wish, and they are only suffering the punishment due to their folly and vanity."

It is better to bear the ills we have than fly to others that we know not of.

THE LARK AND HER YOUNG ONES.

A Lark, who had a brood of young ones in a field of corn which was almost ripe, was very much concerned lest the reapers should come before the little ones were able to fly; so whenever she went abroad to seek for food she told the young Larks to be sure and listen to all the news. One day, while she was absent the master of the field and his son came to look at the crop. " This corn," said the father, " is quite ready for the sickle; so to-morrow go and ask our neighbours and friends to come and help us to reap it." When the old Lark came home the young ones, in a great fright, told her what they had heard, and begged her to remove them at once. The Mother said, " There is no cause for fear, for if he trust to his neighbours and friends for help, I am certain that the corn will not be reaped to-morrow." The next day the Lark went abroad as usual, giving them the same directions as before. The farmer came to the field and waited hour after hour for the expected help; but, finding the day passing away and the corn getting more ripe, and no one coming to his assistance, he said, " We must not, I find, depend upon our neighbours; so to-morrow go and ask our relations — our cousins and our uncles — to come and help us." In still greater fear the young Larks told their mother what they had heard. "There is no occasion to hurry away yet," coolly answered the Lark; "for I know that their cousins and uncles have work enough of their own." The Lark again went abroad, and the farmer coming to the field found his corn spoiling through over-ripeness. He waited for some time to see whether his relations appeared to help him; but, finding that they did not come any more than his neighbours, he said, "My son, let us lose no more time; to-morrow we will cut down the corn our-selves." When this was reported to the old Lark she said, "Now, my young ones, the sooner we get away the better; for when a man determines to do his own work, you may be sure that he is in earnest."

What the Lark said is quite true.

THE HOUSE-DOG AND THE WOLF.

———

ONE moonshiny night a gaunt, hungry Wolf fell into company with a well-fed House-Dog by the side of a forest. After the usual polite inquiries as to each other's welfare and some general remarks on the weather, the Wolf said, "How is it, my friend, that you look so comfortable and happy? I have to work, I am certain, far harder for my livelihood than you, and yet it is with difficulty I can keep myself from starvation." "If you wish to fare as I fare," said the Dog, "you must do as I do." "What do you mean?" asked the Wolf. "Why," said the Dog, "I keep guard over my master's house, and I have the best of meat, drink, and lodgings for my pains."

THE HOUSE-DOG AND THE WOLF.

" Well, then," said the Wolf, " I shall be most happy to do the same; for I assure you that at present I have but a sorry time of it; and to have plenty of victuals and a good roof over my head, instead of my present hard lodging in the wood, where I am exposed to the rain and storm and cold, will be no bad bargain." "Well, then," said the Dog, " please to follow me." Now as they trotted on together the Wolf espied a strange mark on the neck of the Dog, and being somewhat of a curious nature, he inquired what had caused it. " Oh," said the Dog, avoiding the question, " nothing at all." " Nay, but—" persisted the Wolf. " Well, if you must know," said the Dog, " it is the mark of the chain." " Chain !" exclaimed the Wolf in surprise, " do you mean to tell me that at times you are chained up?" " Yes, during the day I am tied up; but at night I have perfect liberty. And then, my friend, I have such nice tit-bits from my master, and all the scraps from the servants; and I am such a favourite with everybody; they all fondle and caress me——What is the matter now? Will you not come along with me?" asked the Dog as he saw the Wolf stealing off. " No, thank you," said the Wolf, " you are welcome to all your dainties and all your caresses. I would not consent to be the greatest king in all the world on the terms you mention!" and away he trotted.

Freedom even in poverty is better than any servitude.

THE EAGLE AND THE FOX.

An Eagle, who had a nest of young ones, while on the look-out for food for them, spied the cub of a Fox basking itself in the sun. The Eagle made a swoop at it, and carried it off to her nest on the top of a lofty tree; and here she fancied she would be safe from the Fox's vengeance. The Fox on her return home soon discovered her loss, and, espying her cub in the claws of the Eagle, begged of her most piteously to spare her child and to have respect to her motherly feelings. But finding that the Eagle turned a deaf ear to all her entreaties, she snatched a burning brand from a neighbouring fire, and at once set a-light the lower parts of the tree, which created such a cloud of smoke and flame, that the

THE EAGLE AND THE FOX.

Eagle, in her turn being afraid lest she and her offspring should be burnt, besought the Fox to desist, and was very glad to restore to the Fox the cub which in her fancied security she had so cruelly denied her.

Never despise the power of those who you fancy are weaker than yourself.

THE GARDENER AND HIS ASS.

A GARDENER, who was in the habit of going to market once a-week, loaded his Ass so heavily with different kinds of vegetables that scarcely any part of him could be seen. Their road lay through a willow-bed, and the Gardener cut some of the willows for binders, and placed them on the top of the Ass's load, saying, " A little weight like this will not hurt you."   A little farther on they came to a hazel-bush, and choosing a dozen slender wands to serve as flower-sticks, he placed them also on the animal's back, saying, " They are so light you will not be able to feel them."   As they proceeded, the sun got very oppressive; and the Gardener, finding his coat too warm, took it off, and threw it upon the rest of the load. " You will not flinch at the coat," said he, " seeing I can lift it with my little finger."   But just then it happened that the Ass stumbled against a stone and fell, and so great was his burden that he could not rise again.

Neither man nor beast should be burdened beyond his strength.

THE VAIN JACKDAW.

ONE day a Jackdaw saw some Peacock's feathers lying on the ground, and, having dressed himself up in them, endeavoured to pass himself off as a Peacock. He succeeded pretty well for a time, but when he entered a garden where the Peacocks were, they soon discovered the cheat, attacked him with their sharp bills, and stripped him of his borrowed plumage. Upon this he would have returned to his former companions, but they refused to allow him to come among them, and drove him away, saying, " Had you been content with your own rank in life you would have been spared the treatment you now receive."

He that dines with Vanity will sup with Contempt.

THE VAIN JACKDAW.

THE FARMER AND HIS SONS.

A FARMER, a short time before his death, called his Sons to him, and said, " My children, I am about to die; my lands I leave among you, and in one part of the field there is a treasure, which if you diligently search for, you will be sure to find." The Sons thought that he referred to a treasure of gold and silver; so as soon as he was dead, they set to work and dug up every inch of ground. Three times did they turn up the soil, but they found no treasure. At the time of the harvest, however, their crops were more abundant and fetched a better price than any of their neighbours', and fully repaid the Sons for their trouble.

Industry is its own reward.

THE WIND AND THE SUN.

ONCE upon a time a dispute arose between the Wind and the Sun as to which of them was the stronger; and they agreed to test their powers upon a traveller, trying which should be the first to get his cloak off. The Wind began, and blew with all his strength a cold biting blast, accompanied with a sharp driving shower, but the fiercer he blew the tighter did the man clasp his cloak around him. Next broke out the Sun, dispersing the rain-clouds before him, and shining with bright and welcome rays. His warmth quickly drove off the effects of the Wind; and as he shone stronger and warmer, the traveller, overcome with heat, took off his cloak, and hung it upon his arm.

Persuasion is better than force.

THE FROG AND THE OX.

As an Ox was grazing in a marshy meadow, he happened to set his foot on a family of young Frogs, and trod almost the whole of them to death. One, however, escaped, and telling his mother of the sad fate of the rest of her family, he said, "And, mother, it was such a big beast; I never saw such a large one in my life." "Was it as large as this?" said the old Frog, blowing herself out as much as possible. "Oh!" said the little one,—"a great deal bigger, mother." "Well, was it as big as this?" and she puffed out her speckled skin still more. "O mother! it is no use your trying to make yourself as big as it; for were you even to burst yourself, you would not be near its size." The Mother-

THE FROG AND THE OX.

Frog was much annoyed at this remark; so she once more tried to increase her size, and she burst herself indeed.

Do not covet that which is beyond your reach.

<hr/>

THE PEACOCK AND THE MAGPIE.

THE Birds once assembled together to choose from their number a King. The Peacock, with his gaudy plumage, was one of the candidates; and the silly Birds, taken with his bright feathers, chose him amidst loud clapping of their wings. They were on the point of placing the crown upon his head when a Magpie stepped forth from his

place, and thus addressed the new King:
" Please your Majesty, may one of the most
unworthy of your subjects be so bold as to
ask one question? We have chosen you as
our Lord and King; we have placed our
lives in your hands; and it is to you that
we have to look for protection and for
wisdom in the time of danger. If, therefore, the Eagle, or the Vulture, or the Kite,
should at any time molest us, might I ask
your Majesty how you purpose to defend
us?" This question the Peacock was
unable to answer; and the Birds, seeing
that they had been too rash in their
choice, proceeded to select another King.
From this time the Peacock has been considered a vain pretender, and the Magpie
an eminent speaker, among the Birds.

*Beauty and outside show are not to be
compared with good qualities.*

THE ANT AND THE DOVE.

A THIRSTY Ant went to drink in a clear, limpid stream; but falling into the water he was almost drowned. A Dove, who happened to be sitting on a tree close at hand, witnessed the danger the poor Ant was in, and plucking a leaf, she let it drop into the water close to him; the Ant immediately climbed to the top, and was wafted safely to the bank. Not long after, as a Fowler was spreading his net with a view to ensnare the Dove, the Ant, perceiving his object, bit him in the heel, which made the man give so sudden a start that the Dove took the alarm and flew away.

One good turn deserves another.

THE ANGLER AND THE LITTLE FISH.

An Angler after toiling the whole day caught only one little Perch. He was just about to put it into his basket, when it opened its mouth, and begged the man to cast it into the stream again : " At present I am so small," said the Fish, " I am sure you cannot make a meal of me. If I remain some time longer in the river, I shall become larger and more worth eating, and then you can come again and catch me." " Yes, that may be," said the Angler; " but as I do not like to give up a certainty for an uncertainty, now that I have caught you I shall keep you."

A bird in hand is worth two in the bush.

THE FOX WITHOUT A TAIL.

A Fox who had been caught in a trap was very glad to save his life by the loss of his magnificent tail; but when he went into society again, he was so ashamed of his defect that he became quite weary of his life. However, as he could not recover his tail, he determined to make the best of a bad matter; so he called a meeting of the rest of the Foxes, and proposed to them that they should follow his example. " What is the use of tails?" said he; " they are ugly, draggling, unnecessary appendages; and it is astonishing that we Foxes have put up with them so long. You have no idea of the comfort and ease of being without them; for my own part, I

THE FOX WITHOUT A TAIL.

have never been so active and so brisk as I
have since I got rid of my tail.   I therefore propose, my brethren, that you should
profit by my experience, and that from
this day you should get rid of your tails."
Upon this a sly old thief of a Fox, who
had formed a shrewd idea as to the reason
of the loss of the Fox's tail, stepped forward
and said, "It strikes me, my friend, that you
have found it convenient to part with your
tail; and when we are in similar circum-
stances, perhaps we shall be happy to do
the same."

*Never listen to the advice of those who
have reasons of their own for giving you their
opinion.*

THE ASS AND HIS DRIVER.

ONE day as an Ass was trudging along the highroad, he suddenly started off, and was making his way as fast as he could towards the edge of a precipice. The Driver seeing the danger, ran up, and, just as the Ass was on the point of falling over, caught him by the tail, and tried with all his might and main to pull him back. But the animal was the stronger of the two; and the man being afraid lest he himself should be pulled over, let go his hold, saying, " Well, if you will be master, you must!" Immediately the Ass fell over the precipice, and was dashed to pieces.

Wilfulness will have its way.

THE CROW AND THE PITCHER.

A Crow, ready to die with thirst, saw at a distance a Pitcher standing by a well. He flew with joy towards it, but how great was his disappointment, to find that though there was some water in it, it was so low, that with all his straining and stretching, he was not able to reach it! He then tried to break the Pitcher, or to overturn it; but he was not strong enough: at last he thought of a plan. Seeing some pebbles lying near, he dropped a great number of them, one by one, into the Pitcher, till, by degrees, the water rose to the brim, and he was able to quench his thirst.

Never give up at a difficulty — try to overcome it.

THE CROW AND THE PITCHER.

THE FOX AND THE WOODMAN.

A Fox, being closely pursued by the Hounds and well-nigh worn out, came up to a man cutting wood, and asked if he would show him any spot where he might hide himself. The man told him that he might conceal himself in his hut; accordingly he crept in and hid himself in a corner. Very soon the Hunters came up, who asked the man if he knew where the Fox was: he said he did not, but at the same moment he pointed his finger to the place where the Fox lay concealed. The Hunters, however, did not understand what the man meant, and so went on their way. As soon as they were out of sight, the Fox began to march off. The man said, "Is this the way you repay me for saving your life?" "Save my life, indeed!" said the Fox, "where would my life have been had the Hunters understood your fingers as well as they did your voice?"

The charm of an obligation lies in the manner of doing it.

THE DROWNING BOY.

A Boy went one day to bathe in a river, and having got out of his depth, he began to sink. Seeing a man passing by, he loudly called for help. The man began to lecture him on his rashness, when the Boy, finding himself growing weaker, called out, "Save me now, and scold me afterwards."

There is a time for everything.

THE SHEPHERD BOY AND THE WOLF.

A SHEPHERD-BOY, who tended his sheep in a meadow adjoining a village, was in the habit of amusing himself by crying out "A Wolf! a Wolf!" as if a Wolf were attacking his sheep. This trick succeeded several times. The inhabitants of the village, leaving their work, came running to his assistance with axes and clubs to destroy the Wolf: but as each time they found that the Boy was only laughing at them, they resolved for the future to pay no attention to his cries. One day the Wolf did come indeed; and the Boy cried lustily, "The Wolf! The Wolf! Help! Help!" but it was all to no purpose, as his neighbours thought he was only at his old game

THE SHEPHERD-BOY AND THE WOLF.

again. So the Sheep were devoured by
the Wolf.

*Liars are not believed even when they tell
the truth.*

THE BOY AND THE ECHO.

A LITTLE Boy one day went into a meadow
close to a wood where there was an Echo.
He happened to call out "Halloa!" and
was directly answered by what he thought
was another boy saying "Halloa!" He
was much surprised at this, and called out,
"Who are you?" The Echo answered,
"Who are you?" The Boy cried out,
"You are a silly fellow!" and "silly fellow" was returned by the Echo. Upon

this, the little Boy got very angry and called the person who answered him many hard names. As he spoke, however, so was he answered. At length he resolved to find the boy in the wood in order to take his revenge, but after looking for some time he gave up the pursuit. When he got home he told his Mother about the naughty boy in the wood who had called him the bad names. The Mother said, "You have only yourself to blame. You have heard nothing but your own words. If you had spoken kind words, you would have had kind words returned to you."

The conduct of others towards us is in a great measure governed by our behaviour towards them.

THE TWO RATS, THE FOX, AND THE EGG.

Two Rats, while searching for food, found an Egg. They were much rejoiced at this discovery, and were just about to divide the spoil, when, to their dismay, they spied the face of a Fox peeping behind some bushes. " We must not lose our Egg," said the Rats; " we must manage to place it in safety as soon as possible. But how are we to do it? Pack it up, and carry it with our forefeet? That will take too much time. Shall we roll it along? No, it may be broken." At last a bright idea struck them. The Fox was still at some distance and their nest was near; so one of them laid himself on his back, took the Egg between his paws, and allowed the other to drag him along by the tail. With a few jolts and some slight bruises they succeeded in bringing the Egg safely to their nest.

The instinct of animals is often equal to the reason of man.

THE MONKEY AND THE MISER.

A MISER, who was as hard-hearted as he was rich, used to keep a Monkey for a companion. One day when the Miser was out of the way the Monkey got upon the chests of money, and commenced throwing the silver and the gold by handfuls out of the window into the street. The people, who saw this, ran in numbers to the spot, and they scrambled and fought for the money and picked up as much as they could get. Just when the chests were almost emptied, the Miser came into the street; and who can paint his horror when he saw what the Monkey was doing? He raved and tore his hair, and uttered all manner of threats against the beast. But a neighbour said to him, " Be calm, man ; it may be foolish to throw away money like this Monkey ; but it is worse to lock it up in chests and let it lie idle as you have done."

A miser is as bad as a spendthrift.

THE FARMER AND HIS DOGS.

ONE very severe winter, a Farmer was confined to his farm-house by the quantity of
snow which had fallen, and being unable
to procure any other food, was obliged to
eat his own Sheep. When these were con-
sumed, and there was no change in the se-
verity of the weather, he ate up his Goats.
After them, as it was still impossible for
him to get from his house, he was com-
pelled to kill his Plough-Oxen. When the
Dogs saw this, they said to one another,
"It will be our turn next, so let us be
off at once; for since the Oxen have not
been spared, it is not likely that we shall
escape."

Take warning from the fate of others.

THE ASS, THE COCK, AND THE LION.

As an Ass and a Cock were feeding together, a lordly Lion passed by, who, as soon as he cast his eyes on the Ass, resolved to make a meal of him. The Lion, it is said, has a great horror of the crowing of a Cock; and it happened that, just as the Lion was in the act of springing on the Ass, the Cock sent forth a loud and shrill crow. The Lion straightway took to his heels as fast as he possibly could; when the Ass saw this, he fancied that it was through fear of him. He therefore plucked up courage, and followed the Royal Beast. But the Lion turning round, and seeing who it was that was running after him,

THE ASS, THE COCK, AND THE LION.

stopped in his flight, laid hold of the poor Ass, and soon tore him in pieces.

Presumption and self-conceit often end in ruin.

THE GOAT AND THE GLASS.

As a Lady was going to church one morning she said to her Maid, " Be very careful about the house during my absence; and be sure if you go into the street or into the garden to close the door after you."   Soon afterwards the Maid, having cleaned her rooms, went out to the well, and left the door wide open.   " My mistress is too careful," said she; " there is no one to be seen in the streets."   But while she was gossiping with another Maid at the well, a Goat, spying the door open, ran up the stairs into the Lady's room. Now in this room there was a large looking-glass, which reached nearly to the floor. The Goat seeing himself in the glass thought it was another Goat, and butted at him with his horns. The Goat in the glass showed fight too, on which the real Goat rushed at his reflection with such violence that the looking-glass was shivered into ten thousand pieces. Just then the Maid came back, and hearing the great crash rushed to the room, and drove the Goat out of the house. But that could not put the glass together again. When the Mistress returned home, and learned the damage which had been done, she immediately sent the Maid about her business.

The disobedient usually suffer for their fault.

THE TRAVELLERS AND THE BEAR.

Two men were travelling together through a wood, which was much infested with wild beasts; so they agreed to stand by each other in the case of any sudden danger. They had not proceeded far before a savage Bear rushed out upon them. One of them, forgetting his companion and his promises, immediately ran to a tree and climbed up into its branches; the other, thus left to himself, felt that he had no chance against the Bear, and remembering that he had heard that that animal will not touch a dead body, he threw himself flat on his face, and pretended to be dead. The Bear came up to him as he thus lay, smelt and sniffed at him all over, and at

THE TRAVELLERS AND THE BEAR.

length feeling satisfied that there was no life in the body before him, walked back again into the wood. Upon this the coward descended from his hiding-place, and asked with a smile of his companion what it was that the Bear had whispered to him; "for I noticed," said he, "that he put his mouth very close to your ear." "Why," replied the other, "he gave me this very sensible piece of advice,—never to trust those who in the hour of trial refuse to stand by their friends."

A false friend is worse than an open foe.

THE TWO HORSES.

Two Horses met by chance near a wood, the one was laden with a sack of flour, the

other was the bearer of a large sum of
money. The latter, proud of his burden,
ambled along with head erect, filling the
air with his neighings. "Wretched slave
of a miller," said he, "get out of my way!
dost not thou see that I carry a treasure?"
"A treasure!" calmly replied the other; "I
wish you much joy of it,—I never was so
highly honoured—flour has been my cus-
tomary load." At that moment a band of
robbers rushed out of the wood, who
seized the Horse laden with the money and
eased him of it; while they permitted the
other to pass on untouched. "Brother,"
said the miller's Horse, "where is now your
treasure? You are poorer than I am. If
like me you had carried humble flour, you
would now have been travelling in safety."

*That which we are proud of is oft-times
the cause of our misfortunes.*

THE LION, THE BEAR, AND THE FOX.

A LION and a Bear, while roaming in the Forest, found the carcass of a Fawn; and a question arose as to which of them had the best title to it. Not being able to settle the matter in a friendly way, they fell to blows. The contest was long and severe, at length both were so faint with loss of blood that they lay panting on the ground quite exhausted. A Fox seeing their helplessness, stepped in between them and carried off the prize. "Ah!" said they, "what foolish creatures we have been! The end of all our fighting has been to give that sly villain the Fox a good dinner."

Half a loaf is better than no bread.

THE LION, THE BEAR, AND THE FOX.

THE TWO GOATS.

Two Goats, after having browsed in the meadows, went to seek what they could find on the mountains. After some time, it happened that they found themselves opposite to each other, with a brook running between them. Across this a plank was laid, but so narrow was it that two weasels would have had some difficulty in going over abreast. In spite of the danger, the two Goats resolved to pass over. They both placed their feet on the plank — they advanced — they met in the middle of the bridge, and as neither of them would retreat, they knocked each other over into the water, and both were drowned.

Obstinacy often brings its own punishment.

THE MONKEY AND THE FISHERMEN.

A MONKEY, seated upon a tree, observed some Fishermen setting their nets in a stream, and thinking that he could do the same, as soon as the men had retired, he descended from the tree, and began to try his hand. But while meddling with the nets he became entangled in their meshes, and was almost choked: " Ah!" said he, " this is a just punishment! for what right had I who know nothing of laying nets, to trouble myself about them?"

Do not meddle in matters about which you are ignorant.

H

THE WOLF IN SHEEP'S CLOTHING.

A WOLF having clothed himself in the skin of a Sheep which he had killed, contrived to get among the flock and to devour a great number of them. The Shepherd for some time was not able to account for the loss of so many of his Sheep. One night, the Wolf as usual having been shut up with the Sheep, the Shepherd wanted something for his Master's supper, and going to the fold to fetch out a Sheep, mistook the Wolf for one of them, and killed him upon the spot.

Never use deceit.

THE WOLF IN SHEEP'S CLOTHING.

THE FARMER AND THE SHOE-NAIL.

ONE day a Farmer saddled his Horse to go to a neighbouring market; and though he saw that a nail was wanting in one of the Horse's shoes, he said, "It is only one nail, I need not trouble myself about that,"— and rode off. When he was about half-way on his journey the Horse cast his shoe. The Farmer said, "If there was a forge near, I should have that shoe put on again; but still he has got three good shoes, and I daresay he will do very well." But the ground was full of sharp flint-stones, and soon the Horse began to go lame. Suddenly two robbers sprang out of the wood on the Farmer. He dug his spurs into the Horse's sides, but the poor animal was not able to run away, and so the robbers took from the Farmer his Horse and all his money.

Be careful even of little things.

THE EAGLE AND HIS YOUNG ONES.

An Eagle rose with his Eaglets to the skies. "How you stare at the sun!" said the little ones; "does it not dazzle you?" "My children," replied the king of birds, "my father, grandfather, and ancestors, have all done the same; follow their example and mine, and there will be no occasion for you to close your eyelids."

Follow the example of the great and good.

THE STAG IN THE OX-STALL.

A STAG, pursued by the Hounds, in his great fear made towards a farm-house, and seeing the door of an Ox-stall open he rushed in and hid himself under a bundle of straw. One of the Oxen observing him, asked him what he meant by venturing into a place where he would be sure to be seen. "Ah!" said the Stag; "I know I am in great danger, but if you would be kind enough not to betray me, I shall be off again at the first opportunity." The day passed on; and towards evening the man who had to take care of the Oxen brought in their food, but did not perceive the Stag. The other farm-servants went in and out of the Stall, but yet saw nothing. Even the overseer went his rounds as usual,

THE STAG IN THE OX-STALL.

and all seemed to him to be right. The Stag now began to think that he might escape; and was thanking the Oxen for their kindness in concealing him, when one of them interrupted him, saying, "Do not be too sure; we hope you may get away, but there is another person,—one with a hundred eyes; if he should come, I am afraid your life will not be worth much." A short time after the Master came; his cattle, he thought, had not for some time looked well, and he wished to see how they fared. Going up to the rack, he asked why they did not give them more fodder; and looking down on the ground, he inquired why they did not scatter about more straw. He then raised his eyes to the walls, and said, "Why are these cobwebs not swept away?" So he went on looking into every hole and corner of the place. Presently he came to where the

Stag lay, and seeing his horns sticking out of the straw, he immediately called his servants, who soon killed the poor Stag.

The eye of the master does more work than both his hands.

THE TRAVELLERS AND THE CHAMELEON.

Two Travellers who had visited Arabia, were conversing together about the Chameleon. "A very singular animal," said one, "I never saw one at all like it in my life. It has the head of a fish, its body is as thin as that of a lizard, its pace is slow,—its colour blue." "Stop there!"

said the other; "you are quite mistaken; the animal is green: I saw it with my two eyes." "I saw it as well as you," cried the first; "and I am certain that it is blue." "I am positive that it is green!" "And I that it is blue!" Our Travellers were getting very angry with each other and were about to settle the disputed point by blows, when, happily, a third person arrived. "Well, gentlemen, what is the matter here? Calm yourselves, I pray you." "Will you be the judge of our quarrel." "Yes, what is it?" "This person maintains that the Chameleon is green, while I say that it is blue!" "My dear sirs, you are both in the wrong; the animal is neither one nor other,—it is black." "Black! you must be jesting." "Not at all, I assure you; I have one with me in a box, and you shall judge for yourselves." The box was produced and opened, when, to the surprise of all three, the animal was as yellow as gold!

Never be too obstinate in your opinions.

THE ASS AND THE WILD BOAR.

An Ass had the impertinence to follow a Wild Boar, braying loudly at him. The Boar, turning round, and seeing whence the insult proceeded, calmly kept on his way without honouring the rascal with a single word.

Silence and contempt are the only vengeance which should be taken of a fool.

THE OLD LION.

A Lion, worn out with old age, was lying on the ground perfectly helpless and drawing his last breath. Many of the Beasts who had been sufferers by him in former times, now surrounded their fallen foe, with the intention of avenging themselves for past injuries. The Wild Boar drove at him with his sharp tusks; the Bull gored him with his horns; and the Ass, seeing that there was no danger, flung his heels in the Lion's face. Upon which the Royal Beast exclaimed, " It is sad to bear the insults of the strong and powerful; but to be spurned by this creature — who is a disgrace to Nature — is worse than death."

It is frequently the fate of great men to be slandered by fools.

THE OLD LION.

THE LION AND THE SLAVE.

A POOR Slave, who had run away from his master, had been taken again, and condemned to die. He was led out into a large open space, and a fierce and hungry Lion was let loose upon him. Thousands of people were seated round looking at the spectacle. The Lion rushed upon the poor trembling Slave, but when he came near, he suddenly stopped, wagged his tail, leaped around him full of joy, and licked his hands. The people, astonished at this conduct on the part of the Lion, asked the Slave the cause of it. The Slave said, "When I ran away from my master, I sought refuge in a cave in the desert; and one day this Lion came to me limping as if in great pain. I saw that there was a

sharp thorn sticking in his paw. I drew
the thorn out; and after that when the
Lion went out hunting he always brought
me part of the spoil. And for some time
we lived peaceably in the cave. One
day when hunting together we were se-
parated, and I was taken prisoner by some
soldiers. The Lion also must have been
captured; and now, as you see, he is over-
joyed to see me again." When the people
heard this wonderful tale they were so
pleased at the gratitude of the Lion, that
they with one voice cried out, "Let this
man live!" The Slave was at once released, and richly rewarded; and the Lion
always accompanied him from that time
forward as tame as any dog.

*Be always grateful to those who have
done you a service.*

THE LION AND THE BULLS.

THREE Bulls fed in a field together, and knowing that there were many wild beasts prowling about they resolved not to separate from each other. The Lion had for a long time watched them, hoping to be able to make a meal of one of them; but this he had no chance of doing so long as they kept together. He therefore began, by whispering slanders and evil reports, to stir them up one against the other. Soon they became cold and jealous of one another, and instead of feeding in a body, they were to be found at different parts of the field. The Lion had gained his end, and, one after the other, he devoured the silly Bulls.

Never listen to tell-tales or slanderers.

THE LION AND THE BULLS.

THE COUNTRYMAID AND THE MILK-PAIL.

A MILKWOMAN, with a can of milk on her head, was walking along merrily to market, when she fell into the following train of thought: "I have eight pints of milk, which at three halfpence the pint will bring me one shilling. With this I shall buy a hen; the hen will give me eggs; the eggs will become chickens; it will be easy to rear them in the little yard behind our house. I shall take the chickens to market when poultry is dear, and I am sure to have money enough to buy a calf. The calf will grow into a cow, and then I will sell her for—oh! how much!" and she jumped with joy at the thought. Down fell the Milk-pail to the ground! and cow, calf, hen, chickens, and eggs, all vanished together.

Do not reckon your chickens before they are hatched.

THE BLACKAMOOR.

A MAN once bought a Blackamoor, and thought that his colour was caused by the neglect of his former master; so he set his servants to work to make the Black Man white. They scrubbed and scoured him, they rubbed and drenched him, but the man remained as black as before; and, what is more, he caught such a severe cold that it was a very long time before he could do any work.

Do not wish for what is impossible.

THE MONKEY AND THE CAT.

A MONKEY and a Cat, who had been always brought up together, were great friends. They were very mischievous; they cared nothing for a beating, and were always vieing with each other in stealing and other sad pranks. One day while sitting by the fireside, they saw some chestnuts roasting; The Monkey had a great desire to eat some of them; but he was sorely puzzled how he was to get them. The servant having left the room he said to Puss, "I know you are very clever, and are acquainted with a variety of tricks. I wish you would oblige me now by helping me." "With all my heart," said Puss, "what is it you want?" "I only wish you to get me some of these chestnuts out of the fire, for my hands do not happen to be fire-proof," answered the Monkey. Whereupon the Cat, who felt herself highly flattered, removed with her paw some of the cinders carefully, and after a little trouble managed to dislodge one of the chestnuts, then two, and then three, which were all instantly devoured by the Monkey, without leaving his companion a single one. While thus engaged the servant returned and caught Puss in the very act. "Wretched Cat!" said she, "it is you then that eat my chest-nuts!" and so saying she took up a broom and drove them out of the room—the Monkey with his stomach full, the Cat with hers empty.

Never be persuaded to do wrong even to please your best friend.

THE WILD BOAR AND THE FOX.

ONE day a Fox saw a Wild Boar sharpening his tusks against the trunk of a tree, and inquired why he did so, as he could not see that any enemy was near. "Very true," said the Boar; "but as I do not know how soon a foe may come, it is better to be prepared. For when the time of danger arrives, I shall want to use, not sharpen, my tusks."

It is best to be prepared at all times.

THE WILD-BOAR AND THE FOX.

THE MAGPIE AND THE JEWELS.

A GOLDSMITH was employed by a lady to make a splendid ornament for her head, for which she had given him many precious Jewels. The Goldsmith's apprentice was often seen examining these beautiful stones. One day some of them were missing; and the master, suspecting that his apprentice had stolen them, caused his bed-room to be searched, and there in a hole of the wall behind a chest the missing Jewels were found. The lad said that he did not place them there; but his master would not believe him, gave him a sound flogging, and turned him out of the house. The next day the master found that another of the stones was missing, and wishing to discover the real thief, he set a watch. He soon noticed a Magpie, which had been a great favourite with the apprentice, come to the table where the Jewels were, take one of them in his beak, and fly with it to the hole where the others had been found. The master was now very sorry that he had accused the poor boy unjustly, took him back to his house, and ever after treated him kindly.

Never suspect any one on slight grounds.

THE BOY AND THE BUTTERFLY.

A Boy while walking in a garden saw a Butterfly, and being struck with the beauty and variety of its colours, he pursued it from flower to flower. At one moment he thought he would catch it as it rested on the leaves of a rose; at another he tried to cover it with his hat as it alighted on a pink; again he hoped to get hold of it on a branch of myrtle, or to seize it on a bed of violets. But all the Boy's efforts were in vain. The fickle Butterfly, fluttering from flower to flower, baffled all his attempts. At last, perceiving it half buried in the cup of a tulip, he rushed towards the flower, and snatching it with too much violence, the Butterfly was crushed to death. The pleasure that he had looked forward to had vanished, and great was his grief that he had been the cause of the death of the beautiful insect.

The pursuit of pleasure often ends in disappointment.

THE TWO COCKS.

Two Cocks disputed for mastery in a farm-yard. The combat was cruel and bloody, and maintained fiercely for a long time; at length one of them gave in and crept into a corner of the hen-house. The conqueror flew up to the top of the house, clapping his wings, and crowed loudly at his victory. At this moment an Eagle, who was hovering near, hearing him make this great noise, pounced upon him and bore him away in his talons.

Be not too proud of your success.

THE LION AND OTHER BEASTS HUNTING.

THE Lion and several other Beasts entered into an agreement to share whatever they caught in hunting. The first day they went out together, a fat Stag was taken, which was divided into three parts. The Lion having elected himself chief commissioner, laid his paw on one of the shares, and thus spoke :—" This first piece I claim as being your lord and king; this second I also claim as being the bravest and most courageous among you; and as for the third," exclaimed he, glaring fiercely round on the assembled beasts,—" I intend to take that likewise, and let me see which of you dare hinder me."

Might too often makes itself a right.

THE LION AND OTHER BEASTS HUNTING.

THE ANTS AND THE FLIES.

ONE bright summer day a Father and Son were in a beautiful flower-garden; the Boy—as is the habit of little boys—was running about here, there, and everywhere. At length his Father saw that his attention was fixed on something at the farther end of the garden. Presently the Boy called to his Father to come to him. When his Father reached the spot where his Son was standing, he saw that he was observing some Ants who on that sunshiny day were storing away their winter provision. "Father," said the Boy, "what silly little animals these Ants are! Here they are toiling and broiling on this summer day, why don't they run about and enjoy themselves in the merry sunshine like those happy Flies?" The Father made no answer at that time to the question of his Son. Summer passed away, with its joy and gladness. Autumn, with its ripening grain, also passed away. The winter came, with its cold frost and biting blast; and the Father and the Son were again in the garden. But how changed it seemed from that bright summer day! The Father took his Son by the hand, and led him to that part where he had noticed the Ants at their work. He then removed a tuft of grass, and showed him that the Ants were all alive and in motion; he then pointed to the dead bodies of the Flies that lay scattered about, and said, "Had those Flies employed their time in summer as usefully as these Ants, they, too, might have been like them happy and well. And do you, my son, employ your youth in so useful a

manner that when you reach old age —
you may not have to look back on a life
misspent."

*Let all young children remember this,
and try to imitate the industrious little Ants.*

THE MONKEY.

ONCE a Monkey was heard to say, " What
a weary life I lead in these forests with
these stupid animals for companions, — I,
too, who bear the image of man! I shall
go and live in cities with people who re-
semble me, and who are civilised in their
habits." He went away, but he was soon
taken, and kept a close prisoner.

Seek your companions among your equals.

THE FLY AND THE BULL.

A FLY had settled herself on the horn of a Bull, and was much afraid lest her weight might inconvenience him. "I beg your pardon," said she, "for the liberty I have taken, but if I press too heavily on you, I will at once fly away. You have only to say the word." "O Madam Fly, is it you?" asked the Bull. "Do not trouble yourself, you are not so heavy as you fancy yourself. I had no idea you were on my head, and it is all the same to me whether you go or stay."

Little minds are frequently very conceited.

THE COUNTRY AND THE TOWN MOUSE.

ONCE upon a time a Country Mouse invited an old friend who resided in town to pay a visit to his rural home. The invitation was accepted, and the Country Mouse exerted himself to the utmost to make the visit of his friend agreeable. He brought forth from his larder all his tit-bits and dainties,—peas and bacon, oatmeal and cheese-parings, and for a dessert some nuts and a nice mellow apple. Out of regard to the feelings of his host, the Town Mouse condescended to taste a piece here and a piece there; at length he said, " My dear friend, how do you contrive to live in such an out-of-the-way place as this ? I wonder you are not moped to death. How can you exist with

THE COUNTRY AND THE TOWN MOUSE.

naught but woods and fields, and rocks and streams, around you? Can you prefer the chirping of birds and the lowing of cattle to the conversation of polished life? Why, you are quite wasting your days here. We shall not, you know, live for ever. Therefore let us enjoy ourselves as much as we can. Come with me to town, and I will show you what life is." The poor Country Mouse felt quite overpowered by the winning ways and polished manners of his friend, and consented to accompany him to his residence in town. It was about midnight when the two friends reached their quarters. It was a large house in the most fashionable part of the town. The furniture was of the most costly and elegant description; the walls were adorned with pictures by the first masters; and articles of the rarest art and richest value were scattered everywhere about. On the tables were the remains of a splendid banquet which had that day been given. The Town Mouse in his turn exerted himself to the utmost to entertain his friend. He placed him upon a splendid Persian carpet, and pressed upon him all the dainties that he thought would please his palate. The Country Mouse could not help thinking what a change all this was from his humble home and his simple fare, and was quietly yielding himself to the enjoyment of the hour, when, suddenly, some persons burst into the room where the two friends were sitting. As quick as thought they scampered off to a hole in the corner of the room, and remained there, their little hearts palpitating with fear till the intruders had departed. They had scarcely crept out of their hole when the loud barking of dogs caused them to run back again in even greater terror than before. This was too much for the nerves of the Country Mouse, so when quiet was once more restored he came out of his hole, and bidding his City friend good-bye, said, "This life may suit you, my dear friend, and I hope you may enjoy yourself here; but give me my homely fare and my quiet home before all the luxuries you have here."

Quietness and contentment in a cottage are better than luxury and strife in a palace.

THE TORTOISE AND THE TWO DUCKS.

A TORTOISE, dissatisfied with her lowly life, had a great desire to see foreign countries. On informing two Ducks of her wish, they said, "We shall be happy, for a fair price,

to transport you to any country you please."
The passage-money having been agreed
upon and paid, the Ducks said, "You
must take this narrow piece of stick in
your teeth, and hold it fast, and we will
take hold of it at each end and carry you
between us; and as you value your life be
sure to keep your mouth shut." The journey began, and wherever they went there
was a large crowd of people, who exclaimed
in astonishment, "What a wonderful sight!
the Queen of the Tortoises with her house
at her back." "Yes, yes," said the Tortoise, "you are quite right, I am the
Queen." But it would have been better if
she had held her tongue, for the moment
she opened her mouth she let go the stick
and was dashed to pieces on a rock.

*Vanity is sure to meet with its due pun-
ishment.*

THE GOATHERD AND THE WILD GOATS.

ONE cold winter's day, as the snow was falling fast, a Goatherd was driving his Goats to a cavern for shelter and protection. When he arrived at the mouth of the cave he found that a flock of Wild Goats had already established themselves there. Thinking that he might be able to secure them all, he cast to the Wild Goats the branches he had brought, and allowed his own Goats to take care of themselves. When the storm was over, he found that his own Goats had perished through cold and hunger, while the Wild Goats had fled away to the mountains and the woods.

Cunning often overreaches itself.

THE GOATHERD AND THE WILD GOATS.

THE KING AND THE SHEP-
HERD-BOY.

ONE bright spring morning, a Shepherd
Boy was tending his Sheep in a lovely
valley; and being a light-hearted, happy
boy, he leaped and sang for joy.   Now it
happened that the King of that country
was hunting in that direction, and seeing
the Shepherd Boy dancing so merrily he
said to him, " What makes you so happy,
my little fellow?"   The Boy who did not
know that he was speaking to the King,
replied, " Why should I not be happy?
The King himself is not richer than I am."
" How is that?" inquired the King; " tell
me how much you have."   " The bright
sun in the blue sky shines for me as well
as for the King; and the woods, and the

hills, and the valleys, look to me as green
and as lovely as to him. My two hands I
would not part with for any amount of
money; and all the pearls in the King's
treasury would not buy my two eyes. Besides all this, I have good health, and I do
not want anything more than I have.
I have enough food; my dress is all I want
for my calling; and I receive as much
money every year as pays me for my work
and trouble. And do you think, Sir, that
the King has more?" The King laughed
and said, " I am the King. What you have
said is quite right: you are as rich as the
King. May you ever preserve your present happy spirit!"

Contentment is great gain.

THE GRASSHOPPER AND THE ANT.

A GRASSHOPPER, who had sung all the summer, and who had not thought of laying up anything for the future, found when winter did come that she, alas! had nothing to eat. In her distress she applied for assistance to her neighbour the Ant, who, she knew, kept a well-stocked larder. "Pray, sister," asked the Ant, "what were you doing during all the bright and beautiful summer?" "I was dancing day and night; were you not very much pleased with me?" "Very much, my dear little Grasshopper; so you may dance now."

They who will not work in Summer must hunger in Winter.

THE FALCON AND THE HEN.

A FALCON one day met a Hen, and said to her, " I think you are a very ungrateful creature: men are always looking after your welfare and happiness. Day by day they bring to you the best of food; and at night you have a comfortable place to roost in; yet when they desire to catch you, you forget all their kindness, and try to escape. Now I am a wild creature, a bird of prey, and in no way indebted to man; yet when he handles me I grow tame, and never eat but upon his wrist." " Yes, all you say is very true; but though I never saw a Falcon on the spit, I have seen a thousand Hens dressed in all manner of ways."

Do not judge the feelings of others by your own.

THE FOX AND THE STORK.

A Fox one day invited a Stork to dinner, and desiring to amuse himself at the expense of his guest, he prepared nothing but some soup in a wide, shallow dish.   This the Fox could lap up with the greatest ease, but the poor Stork, with his long, narrow bill, could not manage to get even a single mouthful.   The Fox pretended to be very sorry to see the Stork eat so sparingly, and was afraid that the soup was not seasoned to his taste.   The Stork did not make any complaint, but requested the honour of the Fox's company to dinner on the following day.   The Fox arrived at the appointed hour, when the Stork having ordered dinner to be brought in, it was served up in a jar, the neck of which was

THE FOX AND THE STORK.

so deep and narrow that though the Stork could readily thrust in her long bill, the Fox, though very hungry, was obliged to content himself with licking the outside. At first the Fox was very much vexed, but on departing he owned that he had no reason to complain of the treatment he had received, seeing he had set such an example.

Do unto others as you would they should do unto you.

THE LION AND THE RABBIT.

A FURIOUS Lion and several Wild Beasts dwelt in a delightful meadow. The Lion was the dread of all from his strength and

the frightful ravages he made amongst
them. One day the Wild Beasts waited
upon him and laid their case before him;
they said that they were his subjects, and
that it was not right in him to make every
day such dreadful slaughter among them;
they desired that he should live at peace with
them, and they promised that they would
every morning bring him sufficient food,
so that there would be no occasion for him
to hunt any more. The Lion readily fell
in with this proposal; and the Beasts cast
lots every morning, and he upon whom the
lot fell was appointed to hunt for the Lion.
One day the lot fell upon the Rabbit, who,
being at a loss to perform the duty which
had fallen upon him, summoned the Beasts
together and said, "What a miserable life
we lead! We must either be eaten ourselves, or we must spend our strength in
feeding our lord and king. Now if you

L

will stand by me, I promise you that I shall get rid of this cruel tyrant." They all promised to assist him to the utmost of their power. Upon this the Rabbit stayed in his hole till the hour of dinner was long past, and made no provision for the Lion. Now the Lion was getting every instant more hungry and angry; at length perceiving the Rabbit coming towards him he said, "What are my subjects about? Where is my dinner? Be assured that if I have to wait much longer, I shall make them suffer for it." The Rabbit, bowing to him with profound respect, replied, "May it please your Majesty, your subjects have not been wanting in their duty; I was sent by them to bring your accustomed provision, but I met a Lion by the way; and though I told him it was for your Majesty, he took it from me, saying that he alone was king here." The Lion, on hearing this, was furious with rage. " Who and where is he that dares usurp my rights? Canst thou show me where this traitor lives?" "Yes," replied the Rabbit, " if your Majesty will be pleased to follow me." The Lion, breathing revenge and destruction, followed the Rabbit; and when they came to a well of clear water, the Rabbit said, " Your enemy lives in this well; if you will be pleased to look in you will see him." So the Lion went stalking up to the well, and seeing the reflection of himself, which he took to be the other Lion which had devoured his food, he flung himself into the water and was drowned.

Strength is not always a match for cunning.

THE EAGLE AND THE ARROW.

An Archer aimed a shaft at an Eagle, and hit him in the heart. When in the agonies of death, the Eagle turned his head, and saw that the Arrow was winged with one of his own feathers. " Alas !" said he ; " how much sharper are wounds which are made by weapons which we have ourselves supplied !"

It is very bitter to find that we are the cause of our own misfortunes.

THf EAGLE AND THE ARROW.

THE HUNTER AND THE WOLF.

ONE day a Hunter was returning from the chase of a Deer, which he had killed, when he saw a Wild Boar coming towards him. "Ah!" said he, "this beast just comes in time to increase my provision." With that he bent his bow, and let fly an arrow, which wounded the Boar to death. But the beast, feeling himself hurt, ran with such force at the Hunter that he ripped up his body with his tusks in such a manner that they both fell dead on the spot. At that moment a hungry Wolf was passing by, and seeing such an amount of victuals lying about, he was beside himself with joy. "I must not, however, be too wasteful of all this good food, but must make it last as long as possible." Being very hungry, he wisely determined to fill his belly first, and make his store afterwards. So he thought he would keep the best meat to the last, and eat the least delicate first. He accordingly began with the string of the bow, which was made of gut; but he had no sooner snapped the string, than the bow, which was highly bent, gave him such a terrible blow upon the breast, that he fell down dead upon the other bodies.

Death comes to us in many ways.

THE HERON.

A HERON, with his thin legs and long bill, was stalking along the bank of a river in a

very thoughtful mood. The sun was shining brightly, and the stream was murmur-
ing along as clear as crystal, and the Carp
and the Pike were springing merrily to the
surface. The Heron might have easily
snapped them up, but he preferred waiting
till he had a better appetite. "It is not
my hour for dinner, I always like to dine
at the same time." Soon, however, he felt
hungry; he looked about for some fish,
but could find none except some Tench.
"Tench," said he, "does not suit my taste;
I would rather go without my dinner
than eat Tench!" He went on, and he
saw some Gudgeons: "Gudgeons," said he,
"are poor eating for such as me; they are
hardly worth opening one's mouth for."
Thus he let fish after fish swim by, till
there were no more to be seen. By this
time he had grown hungrier than ever,
and at last he was obliged to consider

himself fortunate in procuring a few humble Snails.

Be satisfied with what you have, and do not always be striving after that which you may think to be better.

THE PORCUPINE AND THE SNAKES.

A PORCUPINE, in search of shelter, begged of some Snakes to admit him into their cave. This they agreed to do; but they were so annoyed with their companion's prickly quills, that they soon desired him to leave their hole. "No," said the Porcupine, "let those go away who do not like the place; for my part, I am quite satisfied."

Be cautious in the choice of your friends.

THE HARES AND THE FROGS.

ONCE upon a time, in a park where there were a great number of Hares, there was a violent storm of wind and rain, which made such a noise among the trees and bushes that these timid animals were so frightened that they ran about as if they were mad. And when they thought of the many dangers to which they were daily exposed from Hunters and Dogs, they resolved that it would be better to put an end to their lives at once. With this sad resolution they escaped from the park, and running on they came to a pond of water. Here they determined to drown themselves. As they approached the bank a large number of Frogs, who were frightened at the sight of the Hares, leaped into the water

THE HARES AND THE FROGS.

in the greatest confusion and fear; when the foremost Hare perceived this he said, "Stop, my friends! our case is not so bad after all. Here are other creatures who are as timid and as miserable as ourselves. Let us learn to bear patiently those evils which our nature has thrown upon us."

We ought to take comfort from the fact, that however poor and miserable we may be, there are others worse off than ourselves.

THE FOX AND THE HEN.

A HUNGRY Fox, while searching for something to satisfy his hunger, spied a Hen scratching up the earth and picking up worms at the foot of a tree. Upon the tree there hung a drum, which made a noise whenever the wind caused the branches to beat upon it. The Fox was just about to seize the Hen when he heard the noise of the drum. "Oh, ho!" said the Fox, "are you there? I will be with you soon. Surely that body, whatever it may be, must have more flesh upon it than a lean Hen;" so saying, he clambered up the tree, and in the meanwhile the Hen made her escape. The famished Fox having seized his prey, fell to with teeth and claws upon it. But when he had torn off the head of the drum and found only empty space, he fetched a deep sigh, and said, "Unfortunate wretch that I am! what a delicate morsel I have lost only for the show of a large belly full!"

The Fox himself is sometimes deceived.

THE WOLF AND THE HORSE.

As a Wolf was roaming about in search of food he came across a field of oats, which not being to his taste he passed by. Presently he saw a Horse feeding in a field, and going up to him he said in a very friendly manner, "I have found a field of oats, which will just please you; I have not eaten any of them myself, but have kept them all for you, as I have such pleasure in hearing you eat them." "Indeed!" answered the Horse; "I don't expect to receive gifts from such as you; and I feel assured that if Wolves could eat oats, I should never have heard anything about them."

There is no charity in offering to another that which is of no use to one's-self.

THE WOLF AND THE HORSE.

THE RICH AND THE POOR BOY.

As two Boys—the one the son of rich, the other the son of poor parents — were standing on the sea-shore, suddenly some pirates sprang out of the bushes around, and dragged them aboard their vessel with the intention of selling them for slaves. A storm having arisen the ship was driven out of its course and was wrecked, and with the exception of the two Boys all on board were lost. The Boys escaped to a desolate island inhabited by some cruel Moors. Now the rich Boy, when he was at home, knowing that he had plenty of money had learned nothing; but the poor Boy had been very useful to his father in making baskets. The lad now thought that his knowledge might be turned to some account. So having cut some willow-twigs, he began to make a little basket. While he was thus engaged the savages gathered round him, watching his fingers. When he had finished the basket, he presented it to the person who appeared to be their chief, when all the rest, men and women, desired also to have baskets made for them. So they prepared a hut for the lad under a wide-spreading tree, that he might proceed with his work in comfort. They also promised to supply him with plenty of food. The next day the savages, seeing that the other Boy was idle, desired that he too should make baskets; but when they found that he was not able, they beat him, and would have taken away his life had not the little basket-maker begged of them to spare him. They then ordered him to strip off his beautiful velvet jacket, and put on the other Boy's rough frock, and made him wait upon him, and carry willow twigs for him.

Knowledge is better than House and Land.

THE GARDENER AND THE BEAR.

THERE was once a Gardener, who was so fond of his garden, that he quite forsook the society of his fellow-men. At length he became tired of living alone, and longed for a companion. One morning he spied a Bear walking at the foot of some mountains; the Bear did not look to be savage or fierce as Bears generally are; but there was something about him so gentle and mild that the Gardener at once took a liking to him. After some compliments passed between them, the Gardener made a sign to the Bear to follow him, and led him to a part of his garden where he treated him with all manner of delicious fruit. From that day they became faithful friends; so much so that when the Gardener fell asleep the Bear would mount guard and not allow the flies to trouble him. One day while thus engaged, a fly alighted on the Gardener's mouth, and as the Bear drove it away from one side it would alight on the other; which put the Bear in such a passion that he took up a stone to kill it. It is true he did kill the fly, but at the same time he knocked out the brains of the Gardener.

An ignorant friend is sometimes worse than an open enemy.

THE FOX AND THE LION.

THE first time the Fox saw the Lion he was so terrified that he had almost died with fright. The second time the Fox saw the Lion, though he was still much afraid, he was able coolly to survey him. The third time the Fox saw the Lion, he walked boldly up to him, and talked familiarly with him.

Too much familiarity breeds contempt.

THE FOX AND THE LION.

THE GIANT AND THE DWARF.

ONCE upon a time a Giant and a Dwarf were friends and kept together. They made a bargain that they would never forsake each other, but go and seek adventures. The first battle they fought was with two Saracens; and the Dwarf, who was very courageous, dealt one of the champions an angry blow. It did very little injury to the Saracen, who, lifting up his sword, fairly struck off the poor Dwarf's arm. He was now in a woeful plight; but the Giant coming to his assistance, in a short time left the two Saracens dead on the plain, and the Dwarf cut off the dead man's head out of spite. They then travelled on to another adventure. This was against three bloody-minded Ogres, who were carrying away a damsel in distress. The Dwarf was not quite so fierce now as before; but for all that struck the first blow, which was returned by another that knocked out his eye; but the Giant was soon up with them, and had they not fled would certainly have killed them every one. They were all very joyful for this victory, and the damsel who was relieved fell in love with the Giant, and married him. They now travelled on and on and on till they met a company of robbers. The Giant for the first time was foremost now, but the Dwarf was not far behind. The battle was stout and long. Wherever the Giant came, all fell before him; but the Dwarf had like to have been killed more than once. At last the victory declared for the two adventurers; but the Dwarf lost his leg. The Dwarf had now lost an arm, a leg, and an eye, while the Giant was without a single wound. Upon which, he cried out to his companion, " My little hero, this is glorious sport! let us get one victory more, and then we shall have honour for ever." " No," cries the Dwarf, who was by this time grown wiser, " no, I declare off; I'll fight no more: for I find in every battle that you get all the honour and rewards, but all the blows fall on me."

Weak people should keep out of harm's way.

THE SPIDER AND THE SILK-WORM.

As a Spider was occupied in weaving her web from one side of a room to another, a

Silkworm asked her why she spent so much time and labour in making a number of lines and circles. "Hold thy tongue, ignorant insect!" answered the Spider in a passion; "do not trouble me; I work to transmit my name to those who come after me; fame is the object of my desires. Thou art a simpleton to enclose thyself in a shell, and then to die of hunger in it; that is the only reward and fruit of thy labour!" While Madam Spider was speaking in this wonderful way, a servant entered the room with some food for the Silkworm, and, spying the Spider, she raised her broom, and with one sweep she demolished the Spider, her work, and her hopes of fame.

Never boast of your own performances.

THE HART AND THE VINE.

A HART pursued by some Hunters found a shelter among the leaves of a Vine. The foliage was so thick that when the Hunters came up they did not observe him. They were on the point of going away when the Hart, thinking that the danger was over, commenced eating the leaves of the Vine. But one of the Hunters, hearing a rustling sound, turned round and spying the Hart, aimed at him and killed him. When he was dying he said, " This is a just punishment for my ingratitude. Why could I not have left alone those leaves which would have protected me in the hour of danger ? "

When ingratitude is punished, no one weeps.

THE GOAT WITHOUT A BEARD.

A GOAT, as vain as a Goat can be, had a great desire to distinguish himself in the eyes of his own kin.   He was in the habit of going to a clear fountain to admire his form.   " I hate," said he one day, " this ugly beard,—it makes me look so old." He determined to have it taken off; with this object in view he placed himself in the hands of a Monkey, who followed the calling of a barber.   The Monkey received him with the greatest politeness, made him sit down on a wooden chair, placed a towel under his chin, and shaved him.   When he had finished, the Monkey said, "Sir, I trust I may depend on your custom; you have never been so well shaved before; your face is as smooth as glass."   The Goat, proud of the praises of the Monkey, left his seat, and ran off to the neighbouring hills. All theShe-goats gathered round him, and said, "What is this? where is his beard!" "Why have you disfigured yourself in this manner?" said they to him. "How silly you are," answered the Goat, "you know little of the world! Wherever we go, do not people mock us? Even the very children in the streets insult us, and seize us by the beard. Be advised by me,—follow my example, and cease to be objects of ridicule." "Brother," replied another Goat, "you are foolish; if the children can mortify your pride, how will you stand the laughter of all our flock?"

Those who think too much of their personal appearance are despised by all who know them.

THE MERCHANT AND HIS FRIEND.

A CERTAIN Merchant had a desire to take a long journey; but as he did not know what fortune he might meet with, he left in the hands of a friend a great number of bars of iron, so that he might have some property in case he should come back empty-handed. Some time after, having had nothing but ill-luck in his travels, he returned home; and the first thing he did was to go to his friend, and demand his iron; but his friend, having been in want of money, had sold it to pay his debts. "Truly, friend," said he, "I put your iron into a room, and locked it up, but there happened to be a rat there who has eaten it all up." The Merchant, pretending ignorance, answered, "I am very sorry to hear of this loss; but I have suffered by rats in the same manner many times before, and therefore can the better suffer my present affliction." The friend was highly pleased to hear him talk in this manner; and to remove all suspicions, asked him to dine with him the next day. The Merchant promised to do so, but having met one of his friend's children in the city, he took him home and locked him up in a room. The next day he went to his friend, who seemed to be plunged in the deepest grief; the Merchant having inquired the reason, he informed him that he had lost one of his children, and though he had made known his loss far and wide, he had not been able to hear any tidings of him. "Oh!" said the Merchant, "I am sorry to hear this; for last evening I saw an Owl in the air with a child in its claws; but whether it were yours or not I cannot say." "How absurd!" replied the friend; "how could an Owl, that weighs at most not more than two or three pounds carry away a boy that weighs above fifty?" "Why," replied the Merchant, "you need not be surprised at this; we live in a wonderful country; for if one rat can eat an hundred ton weight of iron, why should not an Owl carry away a child that weighs not above fifty pounds?" The friend, upon this, saw that the Merchant was not such a simpleton as he had taken him to be, begged his pardon for the cheat he had designed to have put upon him, restored to him the value of his iron, and so had his son again.

The plans of the wicked are not always successful.

THE HOG, THE GOAT, AND THE LAMB.

A Countryman was driving a Lamb, a Goat, and a fat Hog, in his cart to market. The Lamb and the Goat behaved themselves very quietly ; but the Hog was like a mad thing, squalling as if the knife were already at his throat. "Why do you not hold your noise?" said the Countryman ; "you split my ears with your cries. Look how quiet and contented your companions are." "Yes," replied the Hog, "they may well be patient; the Goat has nothing to do but to give her milk, and the Lamb its wool; but I know well that it is my life's blood they seek !"

The unfortunate may well complain.

N

THE DOG, THE COCK, AND THE FOX.

A Dog and a Cock who were great friends, agreed to travel together. One night they found themselves in a forest, and while the Cock took up his lodgment among the branches of a tree, the Dog slept soundly at the foot. The night passed away, and as soon as daylight dawned, the Cock, as his custom was, sent forth a shrill crowing. A Fox, who was near, heard him, and hoping to make a meal of him, came to the tree, and thus addressed the Cock, "Thou art a useful bird; thou tellest man that the darkness of night has passed, and callest him to his daily labours. I am delighted to have met thee. Come down from the tree, and let us rejoice and sing

THE DOG, THE COCK, AND THE FOX.

our morning hymn together." The Cock answered, " Go to the foot of the tree, and ask the sacristan to toll the bell." The Fox went to call him, when the Dog jumped up, seized the Fox and killed him.

The wiles of the wicked are often ruinous to themselves.

THE CARNATIONS.

ONE day a little Boy said to his Mother, " O Mother! give us each a piece of garden which we may call our own,—one to me, one to brother, and one to sister, and each will look after his own." The Mother granted him his wish; and gave to each a flower-bed full of beautiful Carnations. The children were all highly delighted, and looked forward to the time when the Carnations would be in flower. But the little Boy who had asked his Mother for the flower-bed was very impatient, and could not wait till the flowers came — he wished that his would blossom before the others'. So day by day he went to his flowers to see whether there were any of the colours peeping forth. But it was all too slow work for him; so he broke open the buds and spread out the petals from one another. When he had done this, he was pleased, and cried out, "Come, see, my Carnations are in flower!" But as the sun shone with all its power upon them, the flowers bent their heads, their freshness departed from them, and before noon they withered and died. And the little Boy wept sorrowfully over his faded flowers.

By our impatience we often destroy those joys which may bring us lasting happiness.

THE WOLF AND THE LION.

As a Wolf was taking to his den a Lamb which he had stolen from a neighbouring fold, he was met by a fierce Lion. The Wolf as soon as he caught sight of the royal beast dropped his prize, and scampered off to a safe distance. The Lion at once seized the Lamb and bore it away. The Wolf then bawled out to him not to take what did not belong to him, and that it was a great shame thus to rob him of his property. The Lion answered with a smile, "I suppose then that your friend the Shepherd has been making you a present."

Though we may treat others ill, we do not like to be served in the same manner.

THE WOLF AND THE LION.

THE COBBLER AND THE
RICH MAN.

THERE was a poor Cobbler who sang from
morning till night. His neighbour, who
had great possessions, on the contrary, sang
little and slept less; he was always thinking
of the best means of increasing his riches.
If a gentle slumber overtook him towards
the morning, the merry song of the Cobbler
awoke him. One day he sent for the Cobbler. "Friend," said he, "how much do
you earn in a year?" "A year!" said the
Cobbler; "that is not my way of reckon-
ing. I am quite content if I can earn a
little every day in the year." "Well, then,
take this money," said the Rich Man, giving
him a well-filled purse; "it may be useful
to you some rainy day." When the Cobbler

saw the money, he thought he had never
in his life seen so much before. He returned home, dug a hole in his cellar, and
buried his money there, and with it — his
cheerfulness. From that hour he sang no
more. His peace of mind was destroyed.
Sleep fled from his dwelling, and gave place
to care, suspicion, and fear. The whole
day he was continually on the watch; and
at night if even a cat stirred, he fancied
immediately that his treasure was gone.
At last he became so miserable that he
could bear it no longer; he hurried to the
Rich Man, and giving him back his purse
said, "Take your money back again, and
let me have once more my refreshing sleep
and my merry songs."

Contentment is better than riches.

THE MOUSE AND THE FROG.

ONE day a Mouse met a Frog, and so well pleased were they with each other's company that they agreed to travel together. The Frog, being much concerned lest the Mouse should run into danger, tied his own hind-leg to the fore-leg of the Mouse. After travelling for some days in this manner on land, they came to some water. The Frog began to swim across, bidding the Mouse be of good courage. When they had got to the middle of the stream, the Frog made a sudden plunge to the bottom,—of course dragging the Mouse after him. The poor Mouse, in his endeavours to get above water again, made such a splashing and such a noise, that it reached the ears of a Kite that was flying

The Mouse and the Frog.

past, who pouncing down, seized the Mouse, bore him off, and carried the Frog with him.

Do without help while you can.

THE WOLF AND THE GOAT.

MOTHER Goat was going one day to the meadow to fetch some new milk, and feeling very anxious lest any harm should happen to her Kid during her absence, she told her on no account to let any one in who could not give the pass-word, " Death to the Wolf and his race!" The Wolf, who happened to be near, overheard these words, and laid them up in his memory. He lurked about till the old Goat had gone away, and then creeping softly to the door, he repeated in his softest and blandest tones the pass-word. But the cautious Kid peeped through a crevice of the door and cried, " Show me first a pair of white paws, or I will not open the door." The Wolf, much vexed at the failure of his plan, was obliged to march away.

We cannot make use of too many precautions.

THE ASTROLOGER IN THE WELL.

An Astrologer, in his eagerness to observe the stars, fell into a Well. " Ah !" observed a passer-by, " you do not see what lies at your feet, and yet you pretend to be able to read the heavens."

Look before you.

THE ASS IN THE LION'S SKIN.

An Ass having found the skin of a Lion, put it on, and going into the fields amused himself by frightening all the animals he met, and seeing a Fox, he tried to alarm him also. But Reynard, perceiving his long ears sticking out and hearing his voice, at once knew who it was: "Ah!" said he, "I should have been frightened too, if I had not heard you bray."

It is not wise to judge a man by the coat he wears.

THE ASS IN THE LION'S SKIN.

THE WOLF AND THE CRANE.

A HUNGRY Wolf was one day eating his dinner so fast that a bone stuck in his throat. He ran about entreating every animal to help him, and promising them a handsome reward, but for a long time he could find no one who liked him well enough. At last a Crane came forward, and with her long bill drew out the bone. She then asked for her reward. "Do not you think it is enough," said the Wolf, "that I allowed you to take your head out of my jaws? Be off directly, before I punish you for your insolence!"

Those who do good only for the sake of a reward, and are cheated out of it, must not expect the pity of honest people.

THE MICE AND THE OWL.

In the hollow trunk of a pine-tree where an Owl had taken up his abode were found a great many Mice, all of them fat and plump, but without any legs. The Owl had doubtless bitten them off, and in doing so he must have thus reasoned: "Mice are so little that they can escape by the smallest hole: when I catch them I am therefore obliged to swallow them at once. This is a bad practice, and it is unhealthy to eat too much at one time, and to starve for a week after. In order then that I may have enough for to-day and to-morrow, I will bite off their legs, so that they cannot escape, fatten them, and eat them at my leisure."

It is well to lay by for to-morrow.

o

THE CAT AND THE HEN.

A HEN was once very sick, and confined to her nest; this having reached the ears of a Cat, she resolved to pay the Hen a visit and condole with her. When the Hen saw who her visitor was she was greatly agitated. "Don't alarm yourself," said the Cat, "keep up your spirits. I hope you will soon be abroad again. Can I do anything for you, or can I be of any use to you? You may command my services." "I am much obliged to you," said the Hen; "but if you will be so good as to leave me, I am sure I shall soon be better."

Some guests are most welcome when they are gone.

THE CAT AND THE HEN.

THE LEOPARD AND THE
YOUNG LION.

THE Sultan Leopard reclined on soft and downy pillows, and lowly flatterers of every kind surrounded him, and numerous servants awaited his slightest nod.   One day a messenger arrived bringing the intelligence that a son was born to the widowed Lioness-Queen.   The Sultan immediately sent for his Vizier the Fox, and on his arrival told him what he had heard. "You have," said the Sultan, "long dreaded this event,—I see not why: the poor orphan is more to be pitied than feared.   Besides, he will have too much to do in his own kingdom to think of making conquests, and will be glad to keep what he has." "Permit me, your Highness," said the

Fox, gravely shaking his head, "to assure you that such an orphan requires not your pity; either you must make friends with him, or you must make him harmless before his teeth and claws grow, for otherwise it will be too late." The Sultan thought there were no grounds for the fears of his Vizier, yawned, and turned himself round to sleep. The whole court passed their days, and weeks, and months, and years, in the same thoughtless enjoyment, forgetting that children in time become men. One day, however, they were startled with the news that the Lion had invaded the country and was rapidly approaching the royal city. All was now confusion and noise, and in all haste the Vizier was called upon for advice. "Ah!" cried he, "we do require now good counsel. The Lion has three allies, Courage, Strength, and Vigilance, who will put to flight all we can bring against him.

The better way is to bribe him to return to his own country. If we give him two or three sheep, and a fat ox into the bargain, we may perhaps be able to save the remainder from his claws." The Leopard thought this proposal too cowardly, and declared for war. But, alas! in the very first battle he was overcome, and obliged to submit to a disgraceful peace.

Delays are dangerous.

THE MONKEY AND THE MULE.

A PROUD and haughty Mule was one day prancing up and down the fields. He looked upon the other animals with contempt, and kept on talking about his mother the mare, and boasted loudly of her ancestors. " Her father," said he, " was a noble Arabian; and I may say without vanity that I am descended from a most ancient family, numbering among them the most famous coursers in the world." It happened while he was thus speaking, that his father, an old worn-out Ass, who was standing near him, began loudly to bray. This put an end to the chatter of the Mule, and brought to his recollection his true origin. A Monkey thereupon walked up to him, and whispered in his ear, " Idiot that you are to forget your father; you are only the son of an Ass !"

There are generally two sides to every question, and it is best to look on both.

THE WOLF AND THE GOAT.

As a Goat was browsing on the top of a lofty rock, she was thus accosted by a Wolf, who could not possibly get at her where she was, " Pray come lower; I am much afraid that you will fall from that dizzy height; and besides you will find the grass down here much more pleasant and abundant." " I am much obliged to you for your kind invitation," said the Goat, " but excuse me if I do not accept it, as I fancy that you are more concerned about your own dinner than about mine."

A doubtful friend is ever to be avoided.

THE WOLF AND THE GOAT.

THE CAT AND RATS.

A YOUNG Mouse, with a smooth velvet skin, who was a great favourite with a Rat, the master of a granary, was one day pounced upon by a Cat. Squire Nibble (this was the name of the Rat) was inconsolable. "Accursed Cat," said he, "you shall pay for this!" Immediately he consulted one of his fellows, an old Rat of great courage and experience, and who had boasted a hundred times that he feared neither Cat nor trap. His advice was, to summon forthwith the deputies of the Republic of Rats. The order was issued, and at the appointed day and hour they made their appearance. "Gentlemen," said the President, "a Cat—the most wicked of Cats —has devoured the favourite Mouse of

our friend Nibble; shall we permit such
cruelty to pass unpunished? No! it shall
not; my advice is, that we unite together
against this base destroyer of our allies
the Mice: what is your opinion, gentlemen?" "To arms! to arms!" the deputies
cry with one voice; "in this alone con-
sists our safety." Immediately they armed
themselves with lances (they were straws)
and advanced in battle array; they were
filled with fury and swore to conquer or to
die. In the meantime the Cat, with flashing eyes, advanced towards them. Nibble,
thirsting for revenge, darted his lance at his
enemy! Puss warded off the blow, soon
routed her assailants, and after having
made sad havoc amongst them, pursued
them even to their holes.

*It is foolish to struggle against a power
which you cannot overcome.*

THE MISCHIEVOUS DOG.

THERE was once a Dog which was so fierce and mischievous that his master was obliged to fasten a heavy clog round his neck to prevent him from biting and worrying the passers-by. The Dog, considering that this was a mark of distinction, strutted about the most public streets, and grew so vain that he looked down with contempt on his fellow-Dogs, and refused to keep company with them any longer. But one of them slyly whispered in his ear, " You are making a grand mistake, my friend ; the badge round your neck is a mark of disgrace, not a reward for merit."

Some persons will become famous, even if it be only for their follies.

THE MISCHIEVOUS DOG.

THE LION AND THE FLY.

"Out of my sight, vile insect!" roared a
Lion to a buzzing Gad-Fly, "and trouble
not your King when he would rest from
the cares of state." "What!" cried the
Fly, "am I so contemptible in your sight?
Do you think I am afraid of you? I defy
you to mortal combat! Quick! defend
yourself!" The Lion, finding that the
insect would not be brushed away, was
obliged to accept the challenge; so to battle they went. The Lion had no chance
against his more nimble opponent, for the
Fly, flying round and round, seized a fa-
vourable moment, and stung him sharply
on the neck. The Lion, foaming with
pain, and his eyes flashing with rage,
roared so terribly that all his subjects crept

in silence to their caves and dens. The
little Fly had not overrated his powers; he
continued to sting his enemy in the eye,
and nose, and lip, till the Lion was almost
mad with the pain. He tore himself with
his claws in his fury, he lashed his sides
and beat the air with·his tail, and at length,
quite worn out, he sank on the ground.
Away flew the victorious Fly humming
songs of triumph and spreading far and
wide the news of his achievements, when,
alas! he, the conqueror, had the misfortune
to get entangled in a cobweb, where he
was speedily despatched by his enemy the
Spider.

*Those who escape a great danger often
perish in a less.*

THE KID AND THE WOLF.

A KID who had wandered from her dam was seized by a Wolf. Seeing that the Wolf had her completely in his power, and that there was no chance of escape, the Kid said, " If my life is to be short, let it at least be merry. Do you pipe awhile, and I will dance." So the Wolf began to play and the Kid to dance; but the music having been heard by some Dogs who were near, they ran to find out what was the matter. The Wolf seeing them coming, scampered off as fast as his legs could carry her, and then the Dogs took the Kid home to her mother.

There is many a slip between the cup and the lip.

THE KID AND THE WOLF.

THE KITTEN AND THE TWO SPARROWS.

A Kitten and a young Sparrow, who were brought up together in the same house, lived together on most familiar terms. Sometimes the Sparrow was very provoking and used to peck the Kitten pretty sharply; but Puss took it all in good part—as friends should always do—and forbore to use her claws. One day a neighbouring Sparrow paid them a visit, and began to quarrel over the seed-box. "What!" cried the Kitten, "will you dare to disturb the harmony of our family? By my claws, you shall not!" and springing on the Sparrow, she devoured him on the spot. "Ah!" said the Kitten, "I had no idea that Sparrows were such delicious eating." And from that time she began to long for the flesh of her dear play-fellow, and one day she killed and ate him.

The cravings of appetite are sharper than the ties of friendship.

THE WOLF AND THE PORCUPINE.

ONE day a Wolf by chance met a Porcupine. "Brother," said the Wolf, "you surprise me by being armed in this manner; we are not living in times of war, but of peace. Put aside your arms, you can take them again whenever you think fit." "Friend," replied the Porcupine, "I do not intend to leave my arms: am not I in the company of a Wolf?"

Do not listen to the advice of an enemy.

THE BULL AND THE GOAT.

A Bull fleeing from a Lion sought refuge in a cave where a Goat had taken up his abode. The Goat endeavoured to prevent his entrance, and butted fiercely at him with his horns. The Bull, though annoyed at this unkind reception, did not attack the Goat on the spot, but merely said, " Do not suppose that I am afraid of you. Wait till the Lion is out of sight, and then I will punish you as your insolence deserves."

Never take advantage of the difficulties of others.

THE BULL AND THE GOAT.

THE WOODPECKER AND THE DOVE.

ONE afternoon a Woodpecker and a Dove were flying back together from a visit they had been paying to the Peacock. " Well, how did the Peacock please you to-day ?" said the Woodpecker; "was he not very disagreeable? and how proud he is! What can make him think so much of himself? Certainly it cannot be his feet; you must have noticed how ugly they are. Neither, I am sure, can it be his voice — how harsh and grating that was! What do you think of him?" The Dove answered, "Well! I must say I never thought of his feet or his voice; for whenever I see the Peacock, I cannot help admiring his handsome head, his beautiful feathers, and his splendid tail."

A noble-minded man always sees the good in his neighbour, and easily forgets his failings.

THE CAT AND THE BAT.

A CAT having once upon a time been taken in a net, was released from it by a Rat, to whom she solemnly promised that she would never again devour Rats or Mice. It happened one day that she caught a Bat in a barn. Puss was for some time considerably puzzled how to act. At length she said, " I dare not eat you as a mouse, but I will devour you as a bird." With this conscientious distinction, she ate up the Bat.

A wicked man is never without a pretext.

THE LION AND ASS HUNTING.

ONE day a Lion and an Ass went out together to hunt. In the course of their travels
they came to a cave inhabited by Wild
Goats. It was agreed that the Ass should
go in and frighten them, while the Lion
should station himself at the entrance of
the cave, and kill them as they came out.
The Ass accordingly went in, and began to
kick and to bray and to make all kinds of
noises. When the Lion had killed as many
as he wished, the Ass came out and asked
whether he had not done his part nobly.
" Yes indeed you have," said the Lion ;
"and you would have frightened me too
had I not known you to be an Ass."

*Whatever an Ass may do, people will
never give him honour.*

THE LION AND ASS HUNTING.

THE FOX, THE WOLF, AND THE APE.

A Fox having stolen a chicken from a hen-roost, was observed by a Wolf, who resolved to get the prize for himself. With this view he went to the nearest police-office, said he had been robbed, and hinted his suspicions of his neighbour the Fox, who was known to be a bad character. The consequence was that the Fox was summoned to appear before the judgment-seat of the Ape. The Fox swore that he had not stolen the fowl from the Wolf, that he had bought it at a fair price, and as for stealing he was incapable of such an act. On the other hand, the Wolf swore, through thick and thin, that the fowl had been his property, and that the Fox must have stolen it. Witnesses were called on both sides, but their evidence only tended to make the case more confused. At length the Ape arose, and said, " I have for some time had my eye on both of you; and both of you must be punished; you, Wolf, because your charge is false; and you, Fox, because you committed the theft."

The wicked rarely escape punishment.

THE COLLIER AND THE FULLER.

A COLLIER having invited a Fuller to live in his house, the latter declined the offer, saying, " I am afraid that as fast as I whiten my goods you will make them black again."

Opposite characters will never agree.

THE RAVEN AND THE SWAN.

A RAVEN who was discontented with the blackness of his plumage, desired to become as white as the Swan. For this purpose he left his former companions and resorts, and betook himself to the streams and lakes, where he was continually washing and dressing his coat; but all was of no use, his feathers remained as black as ever; and as he had deprived himself of his usual food, he soon sickened and died.

We cannot change our nature.

THE RAVEN AND THE SWAN.

THE DOGS AND THE DEAD ASS.

Two Dogs one day saw something floating on the stream, which the wind drove farther and farther away. "Friend," said one of them, "you have better eyes than I have, what is that?" "If I see aright, it is a dead Ass," replied the other; "but the question is how to get it on shore. It appears impossible to swim to it, for it is driven against the stream; let us rather drink up the water; our parched throats will soon make an end of it, and we shall have provisions for more than a week." No sooner said than done. The proposal pleased his companion, and both Dogs drank away furiously till they burst.

Undertake nothing beyond your powers.

DEATH AND THE OLD MAN.

A POOR old Man, with a heavy bundle of fagots on his shoulders, was creeping slowly to his cottage. Wearied with the exertion he was making, he was obliged to lay down his burden. And as he sat, he began to think of the poverty of his lot, and of the hard work by which he got a scanty living. "Ah," said he, "how weary I am of my life! Oh, that Death would come and relieve me from my troubles!" Death appeared at his summons, and inquired, "What dost thou want from me?" "I— I—" stammered the Old Man,—"I beg you to help me up with this bundle."

Man longs for death; but when it comes, he wishes it far away.

THE THIEF AND THE DOG.

One night a Thief came to a house with the intention of robbing it; but he knew that he had no chance of success till he had silenced the Dog who guarded it. He therefore threw to him some sops with the hope of stopping his barking. "Get away with you!" cried the Dog; "I had my suspicions of you before, but your excessive civility convinces me that you have no honest intentions!"

Never be bribed to do wrong.

THE THIEF AND THE DOG.

THE BULLS AND THE FROGS.

Two Bulls, who were engaged in a despe-
rate battle to decide which of the two
should be leader of the herd, were observed
by a Frog from a neighbouring bog.
" Ah !" said he to his companions, " I see
no good will come to us from this fight:
it may be a dangerous matter for us."
" What is there to fear?" asked one of the
Frogs; " they are not near." " Do you
not see, my dear friend," said the former,
" that one of these Bulls must be van-
quished, and that when the fight is over he
will flee for refuge to these rushes, when he
will be followed by the victor, and that we
shall be crushed to death without mercy?'
The Frog was right; one of the combatants
was soon obliged to quit the field, and in

trying to escape he ran into the bog, whose inhabitants, including the two speakers, were crushed to death by his weight.

When the strong quarrel the weak often suffer.

THE GOOSE WITH THE GOLDEN EGGS.

A CERTAIN man had a Goose which laid him a Golden Egg every day. But not contented with this, the man thought that if he killed the Goose he would be able to seize the treasure that was within her; and so become rich at once. So he laid the poor Goose on his lap and cut her up, but to his great disappointment he found nothing!

Be content with the good things which you have.

THE HORSE AND THE LOADED ASS.

A FARMER who had a Horse and an Ass, was in the habit of putting all the burden on the back of the Ass, and thereby sparing the Horse. One day as they were travelling in this way along a country road, the poor overburdened Ass begged the Horse to assist him a little in carrying his heavy load. But the Horse was ill-natured, called the Ass many bad names, and ordered him to go before. The Ass patiently trudged on; but the weight being too much for him, he dropped down upon the road, and instantly expired. The master coming up unloosed the load from the back of the Ass, and laid it on the Horse; and in addition made him carry the body

THE HORSE AND THE LOADED ASS.

of the Ass. So the Horse was justly punished for refusing to bear his fair share of
the burden.

Always be obliging to your companions.

THE WOLF TURNED SHEPHERD.

A' CRAFTY Wolf disguised himself one day
as a Shepherd. He put on a smock-
frock, formed a crook out of a stick, and
did not forget the bagpipes. Thus ar-
rayed, leaning his fore-feet on his crook,
he approached with slow steps the flock.
The real Shepherd and his Dog, and many
of the Sheep, were fast asleep on the grass.
The Wolf tried to imitate the Shepherd's
voice, but the hollow tone at once betrayed

the enemy. All awoke in a terrible fright, Dog, Sheep, and Shepherd. The Wolf tried to flee, but impeded by his smock-frock, he was soon caught by the Dog, and worried to death by him.

Rogues often betray themselves.

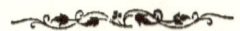

THE BOY AND THE NETTLE.

A LITTLE Boy, who had been stung by a Nettle, ran home to his mother crying, and saying that he had only just touched it. " It was your only just touching it that has caused the pain ; had you grasped it firmly, it would not have hurt you."

Be bold in facing danger.

THE ARCHER AND THE LION.

A SKILFUL Archer one day went into the mountains to hunt. At his approach there was the greatest terror among the wild beasts, who instantly took to flight. At length the Lion remembering that the Beasts looked up to him as their King, mustered courage, and said that he would fight the man, and that they might depend on his valour and courage. While he was thus boasting, the Archer let fly an arrow which pierced his side. The Lion, smarting with pain, rushed into the woods, and endeavoured to draw out the painful dart with his teeth. While thus employed the Fox approached, and bade him take courage and again face the enemy. " No,"

THE ARCHER AND THE LION.

said the Lion, "you cannot persuade me; if the message is so sharp, what must be the power of him who sends it?"

Even the Lion has to give way sometimes.

THE MISER AND HIS NEIGH-BOUR.

A MISER wished to hide his money in some secure place. He therefore fetched a neighbour, a dear friend, and with his assistance dug a deep hole, and placed the treasure in it. Some weeks afterwards, having an inclination to look at his gold, the Miser opened the hole,—but it was empty! "Ah!" said he, "this must have been my neighbour." So he went to him as if he knew nothing. "My dear friend," said he, "help me to-morrow to dig the hole larger that I may still add another sum." His kind friend, desiring to pocket this sum also, replaced all that he had stolen, and waited eagerly for the next morning. But long before the day had dawned, the old Miser had gone to see whether his stratagem had succeeded, and finding his treasure in the hole he took it home, and resolved never again to have a hoard.

The love of money is the root of all evil.

THE MICE IN COUNCIL.

ONCE upon a time the Mice being much annoyed by the enmity of a Cat, resolved to call a meeting to see whether any means could be devised of getting rid of their cruel foe. At this council many plans were proposed and rejected; at last a young Mouse rose up and proposed that a bell should be hung round the Cat's neck, so that they might have timely notice of her approach, and so escape the coming danger. This proposal was loudly applauded, and at once agreed to by all. Upon this a sage old Mouse who had hitherto taken no part in the proceedings slowly rose, and, after silence had been gained, said, "The proposal which has just been made by my young friend is a most ingenious one, and

THE MICE IN COUNCIL.

I have no doubt it would prove successful; but," said he, gazing round upon the assembled Mice, "may I ask which one of you will bell the Cat?"   The Mice looked into each other's faces, but no reply was given to the question.

It is easier to propose than to execute.

THE WOLF AND THE HORSE.

In the spring-time, a hungry Wolf came out of a forest into a meadow, where, to his great joy, he saw a Horse quietly grazing. "Ah!" said he to himself; "you would make me an excellent meal.   I wish you were a Sheep, and then I should stand upon no ceremony, but with you I must be cautious what I am about."   Approaching

with a solemn step, he told the Horse that
he was a physician, that he had travelled
in foreign parts, that he knew the virtues of
all roots and herbs, that he was acquainted
with all the diseases which afflict Horses;
and if his services could be of any use to
him, he would be most happy to employ
them; "for," said he, "I conclude you are
not quite well, seeing you are put out to
grass." "Yes, I have a bad swelling in my
foot," said the Horse. "Then allow me
immediately to apply a dressing to it," said
the Wolf. The Horse, who had begun
to suspect the self-styled physician, allowed
him to come close to his hind-feet, when
he sent forth such a kick as sent the Wolf
sprawling to some distance with jawbone
broken and teeth knocked out.

*He that is a butcher should not pretend to
be a physician.*

THE HORSE AND THE STAG.

A HORSE and a Stag fed in a meadow together, but having quarrelled with each other, the Stag with his sharp horns drove the Horse out of the field. The Horse, anxious to have his revenge, asked a Man to assist him to punish the Stag. "Certainly," said the Man; "only let me put a bit in your mouth and a saddle upon your back, and you will soon be avenged." The Horse suffered him to do as he wished, and very soon the Stag was defeated. But the Horse was sadly disappointed when on returning his thanks, and desiring to be dismissed, the Man said, "I was not aware what a useful animal you were; but now I know what you are good for, you may depend upon it I shall keep you to it." And

THE HORSE AND THE STAG.

R

from that time the Horse has been the slave of Man.

Revenge is often dearly purchased.

———————

THE FOX, THE APE, AND OTHER ANIMALS.

———————

ON the death of the Lion, the Animals assembled together to elect a new king. The crown was brought from the Dragon's house, and it was resolved that the animal whom it fitted should be king. But though they all tried, it would not fit any of them. Here was a horn, and there was an ear, in the way. The Ape also made the trial, and with many grimaces he passed his head into the crown as through a hoop. This so tickled the fancy of the Animals, that

they, amidst loud laughter, chose him to be
their king. The Fox was much annoyed
at this choice, but concealing his vexation
he approached the new king, and, making
a lowly obeisance, he said, " Sire, I of all
the Animals know where his late majesty
kept his treasures, and as you are his suc-
cessor I shall be happy to put you in
possession of them." The Ape, who was a
great lover of money, ran to the place
pointed out, and fell into a deep trap. The
Fox, who had expected this, summoned
the Animals, and thus addressed the Ape,
" Good sir, you wish to rule over us, and
you cannot govern yourself." The Animals
saw the mistake they had committed, de-
posed the Ape, and chose for their king
one who was worthy of the crown.

Keep your proper place.

THE HARE AND THE TORTOISE.

As a Hare was laughing at a Tortoise for his slowness of space, and boasting of her superior swiftness, the Tortoise said, " Let us run a race, and let the Fox yonder be the umpire." The Hare agreed to this, and it was decided that the race should take place there and then. Off they both started. The Hare soon outran the Tortoise, and began to treat the matter very lightly. " I feel," said she, " rather tired; I think I shall take a nap. If Master Tortoise does pass me, I shall soon overtake him." So she squatted herself on a tuft of fern, and fell fast asleep. In the meantime the Tortoise jogged steadily along, passed the sleeping Hare, and arrived first at the goal. The Hare overslept herself, and when she

THE HARE AND THE TORTOISE.

did arrive at the end of the course, it was
only to find that the Tortoise had reached
it long before her.

Slow and sure often win the race.

THE OLD MAN AND THE THREE YOUNG MEN.

An Old Man, eighty years of age, was
one day planting a tree when he was observed by three young men who were passing by. "Surely this old man can hardly
be in his senses to be planting at his time
of life with one foot in the grave! Let us
stay a while and speak to him." Upon this
one of them thus addressed the Old Man:
"My good Sir, what profit do you expect
from your present work? Would it not be

better for you to be thinking of your end, and not trouble yourself about a future that you will never live to see? That may be very well for us, but not for you!" "Listen," replied the Old Man, "the proverb says, 'To-day in health; to-morrow in the grave!' We cannot be sure for one moment after the other. I have planted this tree that those that come after me may enjoy themselves in its shade; and it is some pleasure to me, old as I am, to labour for the good of others,—a pleasure which perhaps I may enjoy when the wind fans your graves." The Old Man prophesied aright; each of the young men soon after came to an untimely end. One was drowned, another fell in the battle-field, and the third was killed by a fall from a tree.

Life is uncertain.

THE FOX AND THE MASK.

A Fox by some means had gained an entrance into the house of an Actor, and while rummaging over its contents had fallen in with a Mask; after looking at it for some time he exclaimed, "What a fine-looking head! but what a pity it has no brains!"

Outside show is of little value.

THE FOX AND THE MASK.

THE FIVE PEACHES.

A COUNTRYMAN one day brought from town five beautiful Peaches. He shared them among his four boys and gave one to their mother. In the evening the father asked them how they liked the Peaches. "Very much, dear father," said the eldest, "they have such a pleasant acid taste. I shall keep the stone, and try and rear a tree from it." "That is right," said the father; "a countryman should always look to the future." "I ate mine immediately," said the youngest, "and threw away the stone. Mother gave me half of hers. Oh! it was so sweet, it quite melted in my mouth." "You did not act very prudently," said the father, "but yet very naturally and like a child. There is yet plenty of time in your life for prudence." The second son said, " I picked up the stone that our little brother threw away, and cracked it. There was a kernel in it, which tasted very much like a nut. But I sold the peach you gave me, and got so much money for it that when I next go to town I can buy twelve with it." The father shook his head and said, " That was prudent certainly, but not natural or like a child ! May you, my boy, not grow up to be a miser !—And what did you do with yours, my boy ?" inquired the father of the son who had not yet spoken. " I took it to our little neighbour who is so bad with the fever. He refused to have it, but I laid it on his bed, and ran away." " Ah !" said the father ; " you made the best use of your peach."

Do good to others, and it will be returned to you a hundredfold.

THE DOE AND THE FAWN.

ONE day as a Doe was standing listening to the distant baying of the Hounds, and quaking in every limb, her little Fawn came up to her and said, " Mother, how is it that you who are taller and swifter than a Dog, and are able to defend yourself so well, — how is it that as soon as you hear the barking of the Hounds you begin to be afraid?"   The Mother said, " It is so, my child; I know not why, but, somehow or other, as soon as I hear a Dog bark, my heels take me off as fast as they can carry me."

The instinct of animals teaches them to avoid their enemies.

THE DOE AND THE FAWN.

THE TWO TRAVELLERS AND THE OYSTER.

Two weary Travellers found on the sea-shore a fine fat Oyster. Both looked at it with longing eyes, both pointed to it at the same moment, but the question was, which of them should have it. Loud and long was the dispute between them, but neither was disposed to yield to the other. At length they saw approaching them with solemn step a learned judge. "My Lord Judge," they both cried at once, "please to decide between us." With a grave face, the judge heard the arguments on each side; he then swallowed the Oyster, and delivering to each of the Travellers a shell, said, "Let each take his due. Depart in peace."

Law is not always justice.

THE COURT OF THE LION.

His Majesty the Lion determined to hold a meeting of his subjects at the palace, where lay the remains of many of his victims. The Bear, unable to endure the smell, held his paw to his nose; for this conduct the Lion condemned him to instant death. The Ape said that this punishment was just, praised the claws and teeth of his majesty, and vowed that the air of the royal palace was sweet and pleasant. The Lion tore him in pieces for a flatterer. The Fox next approached the royal throne. "Well," said the King, "and what do you say?" "I have got a severe cold," said the Fox, "and cannot smell."

Wise men say little in dangerous times.

THE ASS CARRYING SALT.

A CERTAIN man who had an Ass, hearing that salt was to be purchased cheaper at the sea-side than anywhere else, went there to buy some. Having loaded his Ass as heavily as he could bear, he was going homewards, when it happened that as they were crossing a narrow bridge, the Ass stumbled and fell into the stream; the Salt being melted, the Ass with ease gained the bank, and, now relieved from his burden, pursued his journey with a lightsome heart. Very soon afterwards the man went again to the sea-side, and loaded his Ass even more heavily than before with salt. As they proceeded on their journey they again came to the bridge where the Ass had fallen into the stream. Remembering

THE ASS CARRYING SALT.

the pleasant consequence of his fall, the Ass stumbled on purpose and rolled himself into the water; the salt was again dissolved and he was released from his load. The Man was much vexed at this, and, resolving to cure the Ass of this trick, he on his next journey loaded him with sponges. As soon as they came to the bridge the Ass again rolled himself into the stream; but the sponges absorbing the water, he found, as he journeyed homewards, that instead of lessening his load, he had more than doubled its weight.

We may play a trick once too often.

THE WOLVES AND THE SHEEP.

For a long time there had been a deadly strife between the Wolves and the Dogs who were the faithful guardians of the Sheep. One day the Wolves sent a private message to the Sheep, saying that they would trouble them no longer if they would only send the Dogs away. " Why," said they, " should there always be war between us? Why should we not all live together in peace and friendship? Those Dogs which are constantly barking and biting at us are the sole cause of this continual warfare. Send them away, and we will watch over and protect you." The silly Sheep listened to these proposals, and dismissed the Dogs. When they were thus deprived of their brave protectors, the Wolves fell upon them and devoured them at their leisure.

When children listen to bad advice they are like these silly Sheep.

THE MOUSE AND THE OYSTER.

A Mouse resolved one day to go on her travels. In a few days she came to the sea-coast, where she mistook a bed of Oysters for a navy, and began to pity her poor father, who had no desire to wander from his home. "What mountains, seas, and deserts have I visited!" While she was speaking one of the Oysters opened its shell. "Ah!" cried the Mouse; "how delicate and plump! What a delicious morsel!" She put her snout between the shells, which fell to with a snap and crushed the silly creature.

He who tries to catch others, is often caught.

THE EAGLE AND THE MAGPIE.

KING Eagle and Dame Magpie met one day in a meadow. The Magpie felt rather uncomfortable; but the Eagle was very gracious, and said, "Take a seat, and let me hear the news." Away chattered the Magpie, first upon one thing and then upon another. She offered to go from court to court and observe what passed, and report all to his majesty. Her offer was displeasing to the noble Eagle, who indignantly replied, "Remain in your own low place, chatterer; I will have no tale-bearers about my person."

Tell-tales please no one.

THE CAT AND THE FOX.

As a Cat and a Fox were talking together about their friends and their foes, Reynard said, " I have little fear of my enemies, for I have a thousand tricks to deceive them; but, Mrs. Puss, in the event of an invasion, what would you do?" "I have but one shift," said the Cat, "and if that is not successful I am undone." "I am very sorry for you," said the Fox; "I should be very glad to impart to you some of my knowledge." A pack of Hounds came in sight. The Cat ran up a tree, whence she saw that the Fox, with all his tricks, was unable to escape the Dogs, who tore him to pieces.

It is well to have a place of safety to fly to.

THE TORRENT AND THE RIVER.

With thundering roar a Torrent rushed from the mountains, shaking the plains in its fall; it looked as if he that would try to cross it must perish. A Traveller pursued by robbers spurred his horse through its waters, and soon found out that there was naught but noise and foam. He held on his course, the robbers still behind him, till he came to a calm and peaceful River which flowed tranquilly between its level shores. "To ford this will be an easy matter," thought he. He leaped in, escaped from his pursuers, but sank to rise no more.

The noisy are seldom dangerous; the quiet and secret are much more to be feared.

THE HOUND AND THE HARE.

AFTER a long chase, a Hound at length came up to a Hare; but instead of at once putting an end to her life, the Hound at one time licked the poor Puss, and at another time bit her. The Hare being sorely puzzled to know the reason of this conduct, said, "If you are a friend, why do you bite me? but if you are an enemy, why do you caress me?"

A doubtful friend is worse than an open foe.

THE HOUND AND THE HARE.

THE TWO TURTLE-DOVES.

Two Turtle-doves had sworn eternal love to each other; but very soon the male bird began to be discontented with his home, and wished to see the world. "Ah!" sighed the Hen, "will you leave me to die in lonely misery? What do you want? have you not every thing here that you could wish for,—good living, a warm nest, and my fondest affection? Oh! go not from me!" The Dove's emotions were great on seeing the tender feelings of his mate, but his inclination to travel was still greater. "Weep not, my dearest," said he to her, "in three days I shall be at your side again;" and giving his bride a parting kiss away he flew. It was not long after the commencement of his journey that he was overtaken by a shower, which forced him to take refuge in the branches of a tree; but it was autumn, and the shelter it afforded was very slight. When the storm was over he continued his journey, wet, weary, and hungry, and was right glad when he saw a few peas in a field. He flew with great joy towards them, but he was caught in a snare, and in his struggles to escape he almost killed himself. Scarcely had he managed to extricate himself when he saw a new danger in the air; a Hawk was hovering over him, but happily an Eagle coming up at the time engaged in fight with the Hawk. Having escaped this peril, the Dove flew with beating heart to an old wall, where he hoped to rest for a few minutes. But this was not to be, for a mischievous school-boy having spied him, aimed a stone at him and hit him. Wounded in the leg and wing, he now made the best of his way home, and confessed with shame that if happiness is to be found, it is not in the wide world, but in the peaceful enjoyment of domestic life.

Be it ever so homely, there's no place like home.

THE SWALLOW AND OTHER BIRDS.

A Swallow, observing a Farmer sowing his field with flax, desired the other Birds to assist her in picking the seed up and destroying it, informing them that flax was the material of which nets were made, and that if they allowed it to spring up many of them would be sure to be taken by its means. But the Swallow's warning was not regarded, and the flax sprang up, and appeared above the ground. Once more did the Swallow urge upon the Birds the necessity of plucking up the flax before it grew stronger; but again were her warnings neglected. At length the flax grew up into a high stalk; and again did the Swallow desire them to attack it, as it was not yet too late. But the Birds laughed at her fears and called her a silly prophet. The Swallow, finding her remonstrances of no use, resolved to leave the society of such thoughtless, careless creatures. So, forsaking the woods, and the company of the Birds, she has ever since taken up her abode amongst the dwellings of men.

Good advice is too often neglected.

THE VINE AND THE GOAT.

As a Vine was bending with the weight of ripe grapes, a Goat came up and gnawed the bark and browsed upon the tender leaves. The Vine remonstrated with the Goat for this wanton conduct, but he paid no attention to the complaint. "I will have my revenge," said the Vine, "for in a few days you will be brought as a sacrifice to the altar, and then the juice of my grapes shall be sprinkled on your forehead."

Try not to give cause of complaint to any one.

THE VINE AND THE GOAT.

THE WASP AND THE BEE.

A WASP met a Bee and said to him, " Can you tell me the reason men are so ill-natured to me, and so fond of you? We are both very much alike, only that the broad golden rings about my body make me much handsomer than you are. We both love honey; we both sting people when we are angry; yet men always hate me and try to kill me; while for you they build curious houses, and take care of and feed you throughout the winter." The Bee answered, " It is because you never do them any good; but they know that I am busy all day long making them honey."

Industry in brown clothes is better than idleness in splendid robes.

THE MILLER, HIS SON, AND HIS ASS.

A MILLER and his Son once drove an Ass to a neighbouring market town in order to sell it. They had not gone far on their road before they were met by a number of girls, laughing and singing. As soon as they saw the Father and Son trudging after the Ass, they said one to the other, " Did you ever see such a couple of dull fellows to let the Ass go idle in that manner when they might be riding?" The Father, over-hearing this remark, immediately desired his Son to mount the Ass, while he proceeded cheerfully by his side. After a while they came up to some old men, who seemed to be earnestly debating some important matter. When they saw the young man rid-

ing on the Ass, and the old man patiently
walking by his side, one of them exclaimed,
" Do you see that young scape-grace riding
while his old Father walks by his side?
Does not that prove what I have been saying?   Is not that an instance of the respect
shown to old age by the young of the present day?   Get down, you young rogue,
and let the old man take your place!"
As soon as the Son heard these words, he
immediately jumped off the Ass, and let his
Father get up.   In this manner they went
some distance further along a sandy road,
when they were met by some peasant women.
They immediately bawled out to the Father,
" You are a cruel old fellow to make yourself so comfortable on the Ass, and to let
your poor son toil through the deep sand.
It is impossible for the lad to keep pace
with you."   The good-natured Miller,
wishing to oblige all parties, immediately de-

THE MILLER, HIS SON, AND HIS ASS.

sired his Son to get up behind him. In this way they were drawing near the town when a Shepherd, minding his sheep by the road-side, called out loudly, " Pray, my friend, does that Ass belong to you?" "Yes," said the Miller. "One would not have thought so by the unmerciful manner you have loaded him. Why, you two fellows are far better able to carry the poor animal than he you!" The Father and Son at once got down, and the Son said to his Father, "What now shall we do to satisfy the people? We must at last tie the Ass's feet together and carry him on a pole on our shoulders to market." So they tied the Ass's legs together, and by the help of a pole on their shoulders they endeavoured to carry him across a narrow bridge which led to the town. This was so novel a sight that the people left their shops and their houses to enjoy the fun: but the Ass,

patient as he is said to be, could not endure either his situation or the noise on all sides of him, so he commenced kicking away at the cords which bound him. He soon managed to burst them asunder; and tumbling off the pole he fell into the river, and being carried away by the tide he was drowned. Upon this the Old Man, annoyed at having tried in vain to please everybody and vexed at the loss of his Ass into the bargain, made the best of his way home again.

It is impossible to please everybody.

INDEX.

INDEX.